JANE DAVEY'S LOCKET

WELCOME TO HELL #8 ~ HELL CRUISE ADVENTURE

EVE LANGLAIS

Copyright © 2019/2020, Eve Langlais

Cover Art © Dreams2Media 2020

www.EveLanglais.com

EBook ISBN: 978 177 384 125 0

Print ISBN: 978 177 384 126 7

ALL RIGHTS RESERVED

This book is a work of fiction and the characters, events and dialogue found within the story are of the author's imagination and are not to be construed as real. Any resemblance to actual events or persons, either living or deceased, is completely coincidental.

No part of this book may be reproduced or shared in any form or by any means, electronic or mechanical, including but not limited to digital copying, file sharing, audio recording, email and printing without permission in writing from the author.

1

JANE: BUT OFFICER, IT WAS JUSTIFIED…

"Have you seen my locket?" I asked as I scrounged through the many layers of crap on my dresser. And by crap, I mean my hoarding of every knickknack I'd ever collected in my life.

The chipped black and white porcelain kitten my mom had given me when she announced I could not have a real one because she was allergic. The broken jewelry box—gifted by my dad—that no longer played music no matter how hard you cranked the brass knob, the ballerina atop the lid, her tutu ragged. The outside of it appeared no better, with peeling stickers from my youth including some truly ancient scratch and sniff. The inside wasn't any more impressive, holding a plastic ring that had come out of a vending machine, a necklace with my birthstone, and a few sets of discreet studs for my ears.

A modest collection for me. Unlike Grandma, who had a dresser taller than she was—which wasn't saying much, given that she didn't quite make five feet—to store her goodies. She had a penchant for dangly earrings to match the holidays. A good number of them blinked with lights, and I could always hear her coming when she wore the ones that played *Carol of the Bells*.

Good thing I loved the crazy old witch. And I loved the damned locket I couldn't find. It should have been on top of the pile. I'd only removed it that morning to take a shower, but then I'd forgotten to put it back on because I was running late. Finding a way to bun my hair without looking as if I'd slept with my finger in a socket proved challenging, and I blamed Petra. The damned house fairy probably stole my brush again. I really hoped that it wasn't for the hair on another voodoo doll. Last time, the backlash of Petra's spell almost got me kicked out of school.

And what did Petra do when I came home ranting about the essay I had to write about dancing in class? She giggled.

The house fairy always tittered. Which was probably why I didn't kill her.

"Where are you?" I muttered aloud. Not the

strangest thing, considering many objects replied back. It was a matter of asking them properly. Oh, and being a witch.

The locket wasn't in my room, and Petra knew better than to touch it. I'd spelled it, and she'd not liked the result the last time it zinged her—she'd hidden in her birdhouse until her breasts re-inflated.

"Grandma!" The word held a dose of warning. Because there was only one person who would dare invade my personal space.

"Calm yourself, child. I borrowed it," Grandma replied with no need to holler. She used a spell to project her voice into the room.

It should be noted that her reply filled me with anxiety. Because when Grandma appropriated things, they didn't always come back. Just ask Great-Aunt Maisy. Grandma had borrowed her fiancé to move some furniture, then eloped with Gerald rather than return him.

Centuries later, the sisters still weren't speaking, which meant I'd never met Maisy.

Just like I'd never met Grandpa Gerald. I'd just heard all the stories, especially the one about where he died. He'd gotten crushed by a mountain when a certain dragon woke up and smashed its way out. *Never wake a dragon*, was inscribed on Grandpa's tomb.

I'm sure mundanes—humans without magic—

would claim that my family wasn't entirely normal. Yet I was determined to be different than the witches in my family line. I would be the one who wore clothes that matched. Who had a job and paid into a retirement plan. Who took regular vacations to normal places like Mexico and Spain rather than the fifth circle in Hell, or the Elven realm, where the disdain on their faces reminded you why you never visited.

Exiting my room, I didn't have to go far in our cozy house to find my grandmother. There was limited space to hide in the tiny home. Enough for Grandma and me. When I was young, we'd often come for extended visits. Well, I did, at any rate. My parents didn't usually spend the night. Daddy couldn't stand to sleep on land.

He also couldn't stand the cutesy gingerbread-trimmed cottage. He said it emasculated him to be seen anywhere near it. I understood his point. With its pastel green shutters, pale yellow siding, pink window frames, and baby blue front door, it *did* resemble that of the witch who liked to lure children. I'd given up on having Grandma empty the front lawn of its ornaments. I didn't think a gnome statue existed that we *didn't* own—and that included the vulgar ones.

Grandma was in the kitchen at the stove, her tiny, round figure swathed in a frilly apron over a pastel pink tracksuit. Her white hair was a mess of wild curls, and she hummed as she stirred a large cauldron, the smell wafting from it divine—which meant nothing. It could be a hardwood floor cleaner for all I knew. Smart people never tasted from the cooking pot of a witch.

"Why did you borrow my locket?" I asked, peeking over the edge.

"I needed it for a spell."

"What?" I tried not to yell at my grandma. She was old. You weren't supposed to yell at old people because they were wise. Which, in Grandma's case, I had my doubts about.

"And they say *I'm* hard of hearing." Grandma cackled, something she did quite well, given that she was a few centuries old. "I needed it so I could use it as the focal point of a spell. I am delighted to say it worked. Which is why you can't find it."

I sighed, a better move than grabbing hold of the old lady and shaking her. It wasn't her fault she'd finally gone senile. She'd lived a long time. Still spoke of the Salem Witch Trials as "those upstart girls getting what they deserved."

"Grandma, you know that locket is the only thing I have left of Mom and Dad." They'd been taken from me a few years ago. A tragic accident. Although I didn't know how someone intentionally sinking my dad's ship could be an *accident*. After all, someone had hit the button that fired the missile. Then again, it was bound to happen eventually. My dad, an old-school pirate, quite enjoyed taking his ship out and reliving the good old days, flying the jolly roger, firing off a few cannons, boarding ships, and demanding treasure. Then doing unmentionable things to his wench—also known as my mother.

If I ignored the scarring from my parents' lusty habits, then I could admit that I missed sailing with Dad. Missed him dragging me out of school for months on end so I could enjoy a proper education at sea—and in the various ports. I knew swear words that would make a sailor blush. My knot-tying skills were without compare. And I could navigate by the stars.

Useful if I ever sailed. Which I didn't anymore. Last time I had been on a ship was a few years ago, visiting my undead parents. Since they had drowned, they now permanently lived at the bottom of the sea. With my job, it had been a while since I'd visited them. But we did talk on the phone. We'd tried a video call only once via a mini-sub equipped with a camera. I'd required months of therapy after. I still couldn't look at a starfish without flashbacks.

"Don't be cross, Jane. You'll get wrinkles."

"I'm trying to figure out why you took my locket."

"Because of what it symbolizes, of course."

Grandma clasped her hands. "With its built-in propensity, it made the magic that much easier to set."

A fearful tightening in my stomach had me saying, "What kind of spell did you cast?" The last time Grandma had done a helpful thing for me—whipping up a batch of brownies for the bake sale at school—I'd ended up being called Mary Jane for my entire junior year. Grandma told the principal and the police that she'd had no idea the mint in the garden was actually marijuana.

False, of course. Grandma loved a doobie with her after-dinner coffee. Just like the school didn't argue with the profit we made from the sale of said treats. All of which disappeared, leading to no evidence and, therefore, no charges.

The nickname had stuck for the rest of my high school career, to my vast annoyance. When I finally hit puberty—late, as most witches do—and came into my own powers? The acne that plagued my taunters just before prom was justified revenge.

"Oh, don't make a big stink about it, Janey. It's just a little love spell."

I ogled her, speechless for a moment. A rarity I can assure you. "*Just* a love spell? For who?"

"Who do you think?" Grandma grinned at me with all the chubby-cheeked, jovial evil she was capable of.

"Me!" I squeaked. "Why on Hell and Earth would you do that?"

"You're getting old, Jane."

"I just turned thirty. That's hardly ancient." Especially for a witch.

"Fine, then *I'm* getting old. I need a grandbaby to spoil."

I swirled a finger at my chest. "Hello, standing right here."

"Will you put on a diaper and let me spoon feed you?"

"Depends whether it's your famous pudding or not." I wasn't completely joking. Grandma's pudding was only made in times of great joy. She'd not felt joyful for a while. Probably my fault for not giving her a grandkid.

"It's time you found someone. I won't be around forever."

That caused me to squint at her. "You're not sick." Declared more than questioned.

"No. But it's time I moved on. This body can't get much older." She held out her hands, the spider-webbed veins on them pronounced.

"You can't leave me." I didn't really have anyone else in my life. My parents, while not completely dead, might as well be. Our visits had to be short, given they couldn't live out of the sea for long, and I preferred to not drown. Staying alive was still high on my list of priorities.

"Oh, Jane. You don't need me. You already take care of this house by yourself, in spite of me."

True. I did the cleaning, the cooking, the laundry. Petra made out like a fairy bandit with what I paid her. She was the envy of her friends with her multi-story birdhouse that was actually a fancy, suspended dollhouse. Every piece of furniture inside was hand-crafted.

"Who will teach me magic?" I arched a brow.

"You already know more than enough. And it's not like I won't visit."

"I don't want you to go." Grandma might drive me bonkers, but I enjoyed having her around.

"I know you don't, which is why I cast that love spell. So you won't be alone."

The groan I uttered proved epic on the scale of annoyance. "I don't need a man. They're too much work." The ones I met just didn't appeal. The humans lacked the strength to impress me, and the warlocks were just dicks who literally spent way too much time looking for spells to be even bigger assholes.

"You only say that because you haven't met the right one. You need to get out more."

"I go out."

"To work." Grandma used the truth. It sliced.

My stellar defense: "I went to the movies last week."

Grandma demolished it with one word. "Alone."

"Nothing wrong with that."

"Except I want more for you than to be a spinster with cats."

"I won't get a cat then." Easy solution.

"You need someone in your life. And I'm going to help you find them. Don't worry. I've cast that spell before with great success."

"On who?"

"Your cousin Flora, for one."

I blinked at Grandma. "Is that why she's mated to four demons?" No one understood how she kept all her hunks satisfied. "I do not want *a* man, let alone four."

"The spell gives you what you need."

Perhaps I'd find the locket in the drawer with the replacement batteries. "What if I need to get laid?"

"Really, Jane. That kind of talk is for whores. We are ladies."

Who danced naked under the moon during Samhain and the winter solstice. Though we mustn't forget the spring equinox and, of course, May Day. Nude dancing was a family rite of passage.

"Did you run this madcap idea by Mom and Dad?"

"As a matter of fact, smarty pantaloons, I did. They even helped with it."

"My parents are in cahoots to get me hitched?" Could my annoyance get any worse?

"Your mother says it's past time you allowed yourself to be kidnapped."

"Abducting a woman and ravaging her is now considered a felony." Despite the fact that my mother romanticized it at every turn.

Grandma waved her hand. "Bah. Rules are for the mundanes."

"I'm surprised Daddy is on board with this." As his precious little girl, he used to glower at any boy who even looked at me. Which, at the age of five, led to many tears.

Since his undeath, he wasn't around anymore to pull forth a cutlass and threaten to make the boys I dated walk the plank. At times, I missed that.

"Your father agreed because he knows better than to argue with your mother."

Who knew a blood-thirsty pirate would have a weakness? Kind of cute…in a gagging way.

"So, where is my locket now?"

"Off doing its job." Grandma waved a hand as she gave me the vaguest answer possible.

It killed me to lose the pendant. I loved the antique heart-shaped metal piece. When you opened it, a picture of my mom and dad was nestled inside.

But knowing it now held a trap, I'd have to do my best to avoid it.

"I'm not going to fall in love just because you cast a spell." I didn't care how good of a witch Grandma was. She wasn't the only one with power.

"You're so adorable when you defy me." Being shorter than me by almost a foot didn't stop Grandma from grabbing my cheeks and pinching them.

"Ow! Stop that. I'm a grown woman!" I could screech all I wanted, she still treated me like a kid.

"You will always be my chubby-wubby Janey," she cooed.

Ugh.

"You know, there's a place you can send senile old witches," I threatened and then forgave her when she ladled out a bowl of yummy stew.

Sipping at it, I unabashedly groaned at the salty tang with a hint of red wine, oregano, and meat that melted in my mouth. Now distracted, I barely paid her any mind as she babbled.

"...we set sail in the morning."

My spoon paused halfway to my mouth. "Excuse me? I think I misunderstood. What sale are we going to? And what are we buying?"

"Sail, as in on a boat. A big one." Grandma stretched her arms wide, which—given her diminutive stature—wasn't really impressive. "You and I are going on a cruise." The pamphlet fluttered from the ceiling, and I caught it, immediately noticing the caption across the top.

"Hell Cruise is offering an adventure on the high seas experience. Not exactly a selling point," I muttered.

"You didn't really expect me to book something with mundane folk, did you?" Grandma's lip curled.

I kept reading, and my brows crawled up my forehead with each new line.

Hell Hub Travel is delighted to offer a new kind of pleasure cruise specially designed for the non-mundane inhabitants of the accessible planes.

- *Expect magical turndown service. Each room comes with its own maid/butler. Freeing them will result in replacement fees.*
- *We offer catered meals* for even the most discerning palate. (*Please advise us ahead of time of special dietary requirements. Extra costs for those requiring fresh, vegan, mundane blood.)*
- *Numerous pools to choose from: boiling hot springs, mud, gelatin, and even a lava tub.*
- *Onboard activities include shuffle head, midnight yoga, and massages and facials from a jar or spat straight from the source.*
- *Exciting destinations. Each cruise through the*

> *Bermuda Triangle will feature numerous ports of call such as Mermaid Bay, Siren Isle***, Atlantis (if it's not lost again) and if the seas decide to tip us over, an up-close look at DJ's Locker.*

***Please note we are not responsible for the loss of any male companions or family members who choose to follow a siren's song.

Relax in our varied staterooms, from windowless for the daylight-challenged, to the opulent Princess Suite with an ocean-view balcony.

I paused in my reading. "I don't suppose you doled out for a suite?"

"Bah. Why spend all that extra money on a room we'll be using only for sleep?"

"You're a cheap old witch," I grumbled.

"The stingiest," she agreed with a nod and a smile. "I can't wait to relax on deck. Maybe spell a few pool boys to rub my feet and grease other parts."

"Grandma!" I blinked at her language. "What happened to being a lady?"

"Really, Jane, get your mind out of the gutter. Nothing wrong with asking for help for the hard-to-reach spots."

"But you implied..." Sometimes, dealing with my grandmother could confuse. One minute, she made pot cookies and wore halter tops with hoop earrings. The next, she acted like G-strings were the most sinful thing ever. Which didn't explain the drawerful she kept.

"And this is why you need a husband. Look at how your mind keeps wandering in dirty directions."

"Not my fault. Blame Mom and Dad. Hard to be a prude when you were conceived in front of a crowd."

"Really, Jane. Must you bring that up?" Grandma *tsked* as I reminded her of my parents' courtship.

My dad, being a pirate, had kidnapped my mother. They'd fought. My mom had refused to give in, which in turn drove my father wild. He had her chained in his room when he left the ship to get drunk in a tavern.

An enemy of my dad's snuck on board and stole her. My father then went to her rescue and slaughtered everyone in his way. Mom said it was the most romantic thing ever.

Things got a little hot when they finally reunited. As in, on the deck, practically on top of the bodies of Dad's enemies, in full view of his crew. Who then all died because they'd seen Mom naked.

My dad has a jealous streak.

Probably why he didn't mind them living at the bottom of the sea. Fewer living men to ogle my mother. And no kid around to insist they wear clothes and keep their door shut when they had sex, which came after the rule I instituted about no sex outside the bedroom. An edict my parents hated. I sometimes wondered if my dad had gotten his ship sunk on purpose so I'd stop cramping their style.

"How did we get onto the topic of sex, anyhow? We were discussing my locket."

"Find the locket, and you'll find your mate."

"I'd rather not. And as for the cruise, you're going alone. I'm staying right here."

"You have to come. I already bought you a ticket."

"But I don't want to go. Can't, as a matter of fact. Some of us have a job, you know."

"No, you don't." Grandma's lips curved into an evil smile. "Didn't you hear? You were fired."

"Since when?"

My cell phone rang. A glance at the display showed that it was work. I answered. Listened to a flat voice informing me that my services were no longer needed, and hung up. I arched a brow at my grandma. "What did you do?"

"I knew you'd try and use that awful job of yours as an excuse to stay home." That *awful job* being that of a bank teller replete with a steady paycheck, benefits, and paid holidays. "So I called the bank manager and told him that you said wildly inappropriate things to me and asked to see my knickers."

"Grandma!" The urge to throttle her overwhelmed me to the point where I tucked my hands behind my back. "I could have asked for time off."

"You wouldn't have." Spoken sagely by someone who knew me very well. "Now that you find yourself with free time, go pack."

Arguing further would prove useless. Surely an opportunity to push her overboard would present itself.

2

JANE: AHOY, MATEY! I NEED A DRINK.

Despite myself, I was rather impressed by the sheer size of the ocean liner, *Sushi Lover*, just one of the many cruise ships available from Pleasure Industries. Multiple storied, it appeared utterly normal to the casual eye. A glamour, of course. When I coasted through its boundary, riding a stiff breeze, I got to see the details that set it apart from the mundane ships, such as the giant harpoon at the stern just in case a mighty ocean denizen came after us.

The dock had a line of people boarding. Suckers. Grandma and I landed our brooms on the top deck, alighting in the pentagram painted to guide those of us arriving by air. The North American and European witches stuck with brooms, a few of them styled in the popular Quidditch trend, but the fellow who'd glided in a moment before us had chosen to use a rug. We moved out of the way just in time for a zooming armchair.

Grandma sniffed at the sight of it. "Young'uns nowadays have no respect for the old customs."

"Looks more comfortable than a stick up my ass," I mumbled.

"Then you didn't use enough lube." The suggestion was thrown to me by a demon who strode past. He spent too much time ogling my grandma, who didn't notice the leering at all.

There was a young lady on hand providing valet storage for our brooms, and an ogre for our baggage, which was only a small bag each. Brooms weren't exactly ideal for carrying much.

The day proved to be overcast, cloudy with a chance of rain. It matched my mood. Not on purpose. But when I scowled, the whole sky scowled with me.

Already, the forecast in Seattle where I lived, showed sunny skies for the next few days.

Enjoy it while you can because I'll be back before you know it. Since a young age, my mood tended to affect the weather. Of late, it had been soggier than usual.

We weren't the only ones arriving. A portal to Hell, resembling a dark rip midair with flame-colored edges, spilled more than a few denizens on board, including more demons with intricate horns and red-eyed gazes.

The golden arch across from the portal had no traffic at all. Snooty angels tended to keep to themselves.

Another circle on deck catered to the winged sort, like the gorgeous dark dragon who alighted, stirring up the air and whipping my hair in all kinds of directions.

Showoff.

A ghoul was assigned to show us to our rooms. He led us to an elevator, and as it moved between the floors, he gave us a brief introduction. "Welcome aboard the *Sushi Lover*, captained by none other than Adexios, Charon's infamous son."

"Er, isn't he the one who lost the oar?" I whispered to Grandma.

"Yes. And tipped a few boats. Don't worry. This thing has engines, and even if it tips, you should float despite what those Puritans in Salem used to think."

The reassurance missed the mark.

The guide continued. "The upper deck, which we're passing now, contains the club lounge for our exalted suite guests."

"Which isn't us," I muttered.

"The two floors beneath that contain staterooms, a gym, and access to the outdoor decks with the main saltwater pool. Then we have the dining level with the ballroom. More floors with staterooms.

The morgue with a variety of coffins, followed by the water level."

"Water level?" I couldn't help but query.

"For the aquatically inclined."

"Why not just swim alongside the ship?" I asked.

The ghoul didn't even blink at me, he just kept talking. "The kitchens serve food all day long. You can order room service for an extra cost."

"Not happening," Grandma chirped. "I brought snacks."

"The evening meals will be followed by music and dancing."

"I'll be in bed." When I wasn't working on my resume, apparently.

The route to our room proved Grandma's cheapness. We weren't just buried in the ship, I could hear the engines rumbling as if in the next room, and I was less than reassured by the lack of windows once we got to our cell.

I did a quick circuit. Quick because the room was just that: tiny. I gaped at my grandma bouncing on the bottom bunk.

"You get me fired, curse my locket, drag me on a cruise, and *this* is our room?"

"Got a smoking deal, too." Grandma grinned. She snagged her bag and began to rummage. "You should change." Advice given as the old woman pulled out a string bikini.

"I'm fine." A collared t-shirt tucked into a tennis skort. Sensible running shoes. My hair tightly braided and pinned in a crown atop my head.

"Then at least find a drink."

"Don't tell me you splurged for the beverage package."

That sent Grandma into a fit of laughter. "Oh, dear Janey. A witch never pays for a drink. You should always charm someone into buying it."

"You know I'm not good at that kind of magic."

"Not magic. Charm. As in being nice to someone. Smiling, maybe flirting a little. Batting your lashes."

"Have you met me?" I stared at my grandma, who sighed.

"You could try to be nice, you know. It's not that hard."

"That would involve talking to people. Not a fan of it."

"You talk to me," Grandma pointed out.

"Because someone needs to say 'no' to you once in a while."

"You need friends, Jane."

"I have friends."

"Who are all married. When was the last time you saw them?" Grandma asked softly.

I crossed my arms. "A while. They've been busy." With their husbands and children and lives that didn't have a lot of room for a single friend who didn't babysit or have anyone young enough to make a playdate. "Just because they got hitched doesn't mean I have to. A woman can have a fulfilling life alone. I mean, look at you, single and rocking it."

"Age is a number. With the proper state of mind, you can be young forever." She primped her hair, the white curly mass wild, and since I'd seen her last, streaked with blue. It matched her bikini.

"This better not be a singles' cruise." I did not need a bunch of horny guys trying to get into my pants.

"No. This is even better. There are about five weddings planned for this trip. Which means, groomsmen galore." Grandma clapped her hands, her expression alight with excitement.

"Oh, heck no. I'm out of here." Dread had me grabbing my bag and heading for the door. One step. It took too long.

A horn blared, and the floor underfoot began to rattle alarmingly. Hard enough my teeth vibrated.

"And off we go! Try and pretend to have fun." Grandma shoved past me.

"Where are you going?"

"To check out the boat."

"What about me?"

"What about you?"

"Aren't we going to hang together?" I asked.

"I love you Janey Waney, but you need to make

some friends and loosen up. Because I will be, and I can't have you cramping my style."

With that final statement, off she went. Leaving me alone. Which was fine. I'd brought a book. I stuck my hand into my bag to find it. The inside proved as messy as my dresser. My hand sank deeper, my arm submerged to my elbow, fingers touching a bunch of stuff, including something moist and mushy. Then…success.

I pulled forth my battered copy of *Yellowbeard*, which Dad claimed was a knock-off of his life story. A favorite of mine. I glanced at the bunk bed and vetoed it for reading.

Going up on deck seemed a better plan. I was on a cruise ship, after all.

Leaving my room, I marked the door with magic so I'd find it again. It took a few wrong turns before I made it to a door leading outside, just in time to see the shore receding—close enough still that I could jump and swim.

Do I really want to be on board a ship with a bunch of single men looking to get laid?

A grown, modern woman knew how to say no. Or then again, I could partake of any offerings, no strings attached, and save the Earth by conserving batteries.

The choice was mine.

The salty tang of ocean air teased my skin with familiarity. How long since I'd sailed?

Too long.

To my surprise, I found myself relaxing in the ocean air, the hum of the ship different than my father's schooner with all its fancy sails. Maybe when we returned, I'd look into getting the *Janey* out of dry dock. The boat my father had gotten me deserved better than to be grounded.

A voice broke my reverie, deep and growly. "Watch where you're going."

"Piss off." Spoken in an accented voice. A peek over the rail showed a fellow with long, braided locks, a battered hat, and a tailed coat sauntering off, leaving a big guy with a dark crown to resume leaning over the railing. A reminder of the other passengers on board.

As if sensing my stare, the fellow turned around and looked up at me. He started to smile. Not interested, I turned away and moved to the far side of the deck when I felt the tug.

Ping. A pluck that strummed a spot over my heart. I glanced at my chest. Nothing there, yet I could have sworn that something had poked me.

Magic. And it wanted me to go somewhere.

As if I'd obey. My lips pressed tight. Being contrary by nature, I moved in the opposite direction and claimed the lounge chair farthest from the others—not that many were out here yet.

I tucked into my book, sinking into the familiar relaxation of a favorite read while at sea. When things got too noisy, I changed locations and heard a familiar voice shout, "Jerk!"

I recognized that flowered muumuu. "Grandma, please don't tell me you're harassing this gentleman."

Her lips pursed. "I am not harassing Shax," she huffed. "Merely indicating that I'm unavailable for meals since we are traveling together."

My brows arched as I punctured her lie. "Since when are you hooking up with me for food? You told me, and I repeat, 'I love you Janey Waney, but you need to make some friends and loosen up. Because I will be, and I can't have you cramping my style.'"

"That's something a whore would say." Grandma lifted her nose and sniffed.

I found her excuses intriguing. Just who was this fellow with his silvered, dark hair and square jaw? I eyed him and his short horns. "Your name…" I tapped my lip. "Sounds familiar."

"Nope. Not one bit. Let's go check out shuffle head." Grandma grabbed me by the arm and dragged me away before the demon could reply.

As if I'd let the old witch off that easy. "He's cute. You going to have dinner with him?"

"Most certainly not."

The vehemence brought out the naughty in me. "Just going to skip right to the drinks and his bed. Efficient. I like it."

Grandma began to choke hard enough that I worried for her health and pounded her on the back.

Once she'd recovered, she squeaked, "I can't believe you just said that to me."

"Me either." I wrinkled my nose. "There's something in the air, I swear. It's making me a little crazy."

"You'll be fine. Why not go find a drink. Get some food."

"Nope. I'm not getting drunk. I'm going to hang out in the room. Catch up on some reading."

"Great plan." Grandma practically shoved me in her haste to get away. I might have been offended, except I preferred to avoid the craziness she was sure to embroil me in.

I never made it to my room, managing to find a quiet spot on a deck no one seemed to have discovered. I nestled into an abandoned pile of rope, feeling quite at home with the salty air filling my lungs. The story sucked me in, back to a time when swashbuckling was accepted, and the world was a more violent place.

The announcement that dinner with the captain would commence raised my head but only long enough to remind me to dig out a snack from my pocket. A protein bar that could have really used a drink to wash it down.

I finished my book as twilight turned to night. Following the spell I'd left on my room and avoiding the leering goblins who'd already gotten into the grog, I meant to ready myself for bed, but it wasn't even nine. Early even by my standards.

The tug at my chest came again. Stronger this time.

What kind of magic was this? Exiting my room, I glanced up and down the hall. A pale-skinned couple dressed in sleek black evening wear went past me, apparently not affected by the summons.

Did the ship exude a compulsion keyed to certain guests? Only me?

The final thought brought a frown. I could only think of one spell that might be for me alone.

The one on my locket. The damned love curse.

"Oh, you sly old biddy." I should have known Grandma had an ulterior motive in dragging me along on this trip. Exactly who had she given the locket to? Someone on board, obviously, making avoiding them nearly impossible unless I abandoned ship. I looked around for the nearest exit to jump ship, and then it hit me.

I was about to run like a coward. Me—a witch almost as powerful as Grandma—afraid of a stupid love spell. Unacceptable. I would confront this and handle it. *Because I am witch. I am strong.*

Shoulders pulled back and stiff, I marched, following the tug to a level booming with loud music. A cacophony of sound that involved drums, guitars, a piano, cymbals, and a group of singers.

It left me cold. Don't get me wrong, I enjoyed music, and especially dancing—by the light of the moon—but the rhythm I preferred to follow had a primal beat. It was the song of the Earth and the moon, the sky and the stars. It didn't have whining guitars or a screeching voice.

Still, if my locket were somewhere on that dance floor, then I'd have to go in. Because only once I got my hands on it could I stifle the spell.

Was a part of me worried that I'd succumb? A little. Grandma could cast some doozies. However, I'd inherited that strength. Not to mention, I had a stubborn streak. I wouldn't allow magic to force me to love someone.

Determined, I shoved at the door to enter the ballroom, only it pushed me back, and I landed on my butt.

At the feet of a tall dude.

I looked up. *Way* up. Into golden eyes staring from a square face with a hint of stubble and long, wavy, dark hair. A good-looking guy built like a lumberjack from what I could see of his thick arms, tapered waist, and huge hands.

One of which extended with a gruff, "Fuck me. Sorry. Didn't mean to knock you on your ass."

Flushed cheeks, embarrassed bottom, and a tingle that found him all too attractive led to me wiggling my fingers. "Then why don't you join me." Only when he didn't fall over on his rump, making us even, did I grumble, "Fucking shapeshifter."

3

OZ: AND ALONG CAME A LION.

STARING down at the woman with her crown of tightly braided hair, I smirked. "Spells don't work on me, witch." A strange quirk of nature that their magic broke apart the moment it tried to touch a shapeshifter. At least, on this plane. I'd heard that in other versions of our world, the rules were different. Poor bastards.

The realization that she couldn't spell me caused her scowl to deepen. A shame. She'd be cute if she tried smiling. The hair pulled back taut showed an interesting face with a pointed chin. Her eyes, a startling bright green, stared at me. I gazed right back. I was also the first to break away because, being a guy, I checked her out.

Upon first glance, I noticed that she wasn't dressed like the other women on board. Mostly because she wore clothes. Her skirt hung down to her knees, her shirt, buttoned to the neck, was tucked in. The ensemble didn't manage to completely hide the curves underneath, though. My smile widened in appreciation—

Her legs scissored around my ankles, and she swept my feet out from under me.

"Ack." Belying all the claims about cats, I hit the floor on my ass and glared at the woman. "What the fuck?"

"Tit for tat, Simba."

I didn't ask how she knew that I was a feline shifter. Witches had an affinity for pussies. So did I, once upon a time. But I'd slowed down my skirt chasing because it got old after a while. Who knew? "Name is Oz."

"As in the fake wizard of?" She bounced up, petite compared to my six and a half feet.

I rose more slowly. "Some say I've got a magical touch." And, yes, there was a shit ton of arrogance in that claim, which meant I deserved the eye roll.

"If I'd known they were letting people bring their pets, I'd have brought my flea circus. They get hungry when I leave them for too long."

"Hate to break it to you, Glinda, but in this modern age, we all get the shots to prevent infestations." Which sure beat those nasty-smelling collars Mom used to put on me when I was young.

"Glinda?" She snorted. "Do I look like a good witch to you?"

"Good enough to eat." Despite her annoying attitude, I couldn't help but flirt. Mostly because I knew it would irritate her even more.

"Please don't tell me that horrible line ever works."

"More often than you'd think." And what did it say about me that those who fell for it usually didn't get called again?

"You should try watching where you're going."

"But then how would I meet acerbic-tongued witches?" I had to admit I enjoyed baiting her. The spots of color in her cheeks and her flashing eyes did something to me. Kept me talking rather than running for my room to hide, which was where I'd been heading in such a hurry.

"It's a good thing your kind is immune to my magic."

"Threats? Already? And here we've only just met. Things are moving so fast. Next thing you know, we'll be throwing cutting insults. Then maybe snarling toe-to-toe." Face-to-face. Lip to… My gaze dropped to her mouth.

It moved and mouthed, "You are arrogant."

"Trait of the species." I couldn't help but smile.

"I'm pretty sure you have some wolf in your

bloodline given you have the manners of an ill-behaved dog."

"Glinda, I'm hurt." I clutched my chest. "As if a canine would have such a luxurious mane."

"I assumed you were reliving your youth as an eighties rocker."

"I'm not that old." But I was getting there. On the latter side of my thirties. Still in my prime, but definitely looking to make some lifestyle changes.

"Are you sure about the age thing? Because you seem to be hard of hearing. Move." She sidestepped to go around me.

Much too entertained and intrigued, I stayed in her path. "Don't leave, Glinda. We're just getting to know each other."

"I know enough. Leave me alone."

Apparently, I craved abuse. "Why would I do that when we're so obviously meant to spend time together? I mean, I'm a cat. You're a witch. Shouldn't you be asking to pet my fur instead?"

As expected, she snarled. "I hope you fall in a pool of hair removal cream." She then stalked past me into the giant ballroom currently offering seventies disco and too many polyester lounge suits.

Being a jeans kind of guy who loved rock and roll, I had made my appearance to please my family members, gritted my teeth and lied about loving it, and now readied to leave. I had no interest in dancing, flirting, or drinking. At least not with strangers. I did have an expensive bottle of tequila in my room, so why the fuck was I heading back into that cesspool of noise?

Curiosity. It'd killed my uncle Bert—because someone did let the dog out. It'd maimed Aunt Gertrude—but spared her last life. As for me, I couldn't picture the witch as the partying type. So what had brought her here?

A straying boyfriend or husband? I'd not noticed a ring on her hand, but these days, that didn't mean shit. Glinda sure seemed pissed as she stalked through the swaying bodies, ignoring the woman dancing on a table. Not easy given she'd obviously cut the hem on her shorts herself. One side was at least three jagged inches longer. Wearing a t-shirt that read, *Best Imp Evah!,* little miss lopsided Daisy dukes swayed to the beat.

The imp flung her hands and beckoned a massive dude, who regarded her with a scowl and grumbled, "Get down from there. We don't have time for this."

"There is always time to dance to *Staying Alive.*" Said with a wink.

Passing the arguing couple, I kept my gaze on the witch. She ignored the trays of booze circling around. Didn't twitch one hip in response to the gyrating beat. Ignored the interested stares that undressed her and raised the hairs on my body.

As if I cared who ogled Glinda. I should warn them to stay away from the prickly witch. Everyone knew they were bad news, and yet, I still followed. She seemed to have a destination in mind. She marched right into a corner where a drunken pirate, who was channeling his inner Johnny Depp, sat slumped, waving around a pitcher of ale while singing off-key.

"Oye, she had a nice pair of titties, a nice pair of titties indeed. And when I put my face between them,"—the word rose in pitch—*"I suffocated nice as you pleeeeeeasee."* The ditty ended with a sip.

The witch stopped in front of the drunken pirate and held out an imperious hand. "Give it back."

I had to strain to hear.

The pirate leered, a gold tooth gleaming. "I'll give you wherever you like, me beauty."

"Must you be so disgusting?"

"You say that now, yet once you get a ride on my peg leg, you'll be begging for more." The pirate gyrated on the floor, no doubt thinking he was sexy. He failed.

It made me ashamed for men everywhere.

"Doubtful." The witch wasn't seduced either. She waggled her fingers and turned the jug of ale into a celery stick, which caused the pirate to stand and bluster as he waved it in her face and yelled at her.

"Bloody hell, woman. Give me back my grog."

"Only once you hand it over."

The pirate thrust his hips. "You want it, grab it."

She crossed her arms and remained unimpressed. "Don't test me, pirate."

"The name is Gaston. You've probably heard of me. Scourge of the seas. Marauder extraordinaire."

"No, you're not." Glinda snapped her fingers. Suddenly, the pirate was clean-shaven, hair close-cut, and wearing a suit.

"What did you do?" the pirate screeched, slapping at his body, his expression twisted in horror.

"You don't deserve the title the scourge of the seas, *yuppy*." Uttered with pure disdain.

"You bitch!" The pirate-turned-businessman lunged for the witch, and that's when my inner kitty nudged and rumbled, *Can we play?*

Hell yeah, we can.

4

JANE: I WILL NOT MARRY MY FATHER.

Irritation threatened to erupt in me. The damned buccaneer wouldn't hand over my locket. And yet, I knew he had it. I could feel the magic tingling in me. Drawing me to this…this…disgusting excuse of a man.

Don't get me wrong. I liked pirates. My dad was an excellent swashbuckler. And I'm sure the one ranting at me to give him back his ale and clothes was the terror of some sea or other.

However, it was the fact that Gaston reminded me of my dad that made the idea of being with him revolting. I'd spent many hours with a therapist discovering that I loved my father and would have to be careful that I didn't try and find a replacement for him.

Now to convince the locket. I caught a glimpse of

it glinting against the pirate's chest under the linen of his shirt. Before I could grab for it, the pirate-turned-yuppy lunged.

Totally prepared to handle it, I suddenly didn't have to. A giant kitty pounced between us and growled. A lion, as a matter of fact, with a dark mane and a powerful body.

Want to bet it was the same one I'd recently bumped into?

More surprising? The fact that he snarled at the pirate instead of me. What happened to bros before hos?

The pirate took offense and swung a fist.

Against a lion. Just went to show his level of intoxication.

Oz batted at it, and the pirate screamed before taking off running—with my locket. The lion took chase, which meant I had to follow.

"Stupid, meddling pussycat." Why had he jumped in? Chivalry, especially after what had happened between us, didn't seem likely.

Perhaps Oz already had a hate-on for the pirate. Lots of people didn't like them, and not just because of the whole marauding aspect. Women found them sexy, which led to more than a few husbands and boyfriends getting jealous.

I should note, the jealousy thing went two ways. My mom had killed her fair share of wenches who dared to bat their eyes at her man. Anyone who ever wondered where I got my attitude from had obviously never met my blood-thirsty parents.

The chase took us from the crowded room, where that woman dancing on the table had just taken a swan dive onto a man who sprouted wings. A beautiful male who glowed and almost managed to distract me with his granite face and the tight curls on his head.

A tug at my chest kept me going. The giant lion chased the pirate onto a deck lit with fancy lanterns providing illumination for those who'd chosen to go for a late-night dip. Sans clothes. Not as sexy as you'd think since that included ogres with back hair long and thick enough to form the bristles on a hairbrush. For reference, I preferred synthetic.

The pirate ended up tripping over a mooning vampire—because that super white glow didn't come naturally—and landed with a splash in the pool.

But the yodeling from the guests in the water didn't arise because of that. Someone screamed, "There's a floater!" As in a turd bobbing along in the shallow end, resulting in a mass exodus, with everyone exclaiming over the grossness. Except for the goblins, who remained behind, expressions smug.

As for the drowning pirate? He'd flipped to his back and slept.

The kitty sat down on the edge of the pool, whiskers twitching.

"Pussy afraid to get his paws wet?" I mocked. I shouldn't tease too hard, given I wasn't about to enter the shit-infested waters. I waggled my fingers —rather than my ass as Mother had advised me— and brought Mr. Pirate to the deck.

He snored. Loudly. I knelt by his side and began rummaging for the necklace.

"What are you doing?" asked Oz, who'd obviously traded his lion shape for man.

"Looking for something." Which I wasn't finding. Tearing open the shirt showed only the pirate's bare chest.

"A witch and a thief?" Oz said. "No wonder he attacked you. If I'd have known, I wouldn't have interfered."

"I wish you had stayed out of it. He has something of mine," I grumbled. My irritation grew as I realized that the locket was gone. No longer around the neck of the pirate, and not in any of his pockets.

Standing, I took a peek at the pool, already turning into a rancid green miasma. Despite the scum spreading over the top, I could tell my necklace hadn't sunk into its depths either.

The tug in my chest was gone, along with my

jewelry. Probably looking for a new victim since the pirate hadn't worked out.

I turned away from the pool, ready to leave, only to come face-to-chest with a very naked Oz. He was ridiculously muscled and impressive.

Oh, my. Forget the good witch Glinda, I suddenly became the scarecrow without a brain.

5

OZ: LIONS DON'T PURR. BUT YOU
CAN STILL PET ME. LOWER.

The moment the witch took note of my current state of undress, her eyes widened, her lips parted, and her temperature spiked. Yet, I was sure she would have protested if I'd called her on the fact that she liked what she saw. It didn't take an educated guess to know she'd probably lie, yet my nose clearly scented arousal. Sweet, sweet arousal.

For me.

Being a man, I liked it. Wanted to explore exactly what kind of passion lurked under that prickly exterior. But I did have a sense of self-preservation, and a big chunk of curiosity that was still intrigued by her actions.

"What did the pirate steal?" I asked.

"Something personal of mine."

"Are you sure he took it?"

She cast me a glance that rebuked me for even questioning the fact.

"Had to ask." I shrugged, which drew her gaze to my body. The scent of her arousal intensified. Was it any wonder a certain part of my anatomy reacted?

Given she'd returned to stare me in the face, she might not have realized it if someone hadn't whisper-shouted, "Fuck me, he's hung almost as good as a centaur."

Followed by, "No, let him fuck me. I like a man with girth."

Which led to the witch dropping her gaze. Her cheeks turned red and, despite her sweet interest, she straightened, and her expression turned stony. "You should see someone about getting that fixed."

"Are you offering?"

Her lips parted. "Why, I never!"

"Obviously, or it wouldn't be so hard." I winked.

She couldn't handle it. Without another word, she left.

I couldn't help but turn around to watch her go, the ass on her as fine as the front. Off she stomped, obviously angry. I couldn't care less. Let her assault another passenger. My bottle of tequila beckoned.

Once more, my feet betrayed me. Me, who never chased a woman, who let them come to *me* for petting, followed the grouchy witch.

Or I would have if a bevy of nymphs didn't block

my path. By the time I'd extricated myself, saving my virtue from their greedy hands, the witch was gone.

And I still didn't have a name. Didn't need one though since I had a scent to track her. What I also didn't have was an answer to why I even wanted to. She'd made it clear that she didn't like me. Her attitude bordered on mean-sarcastic with a hint of acerbic. Going for her? Good looks. However, pretty women weren't uncommon, so why my interest?

Because she smells good.

My inner feline had a simple answer. At the same time, it was the only one.

A shifter tended to make many decisions based on scent alone. Hot, fresh chocolate chip cookies? The smell of them meant automatic, justified theft.

And Glinda smelled even better than dessert. My gut said to stick close to her. My dick thought we should get even closer.

Since my nudity distracted, mostly in the form of people who kept thinking I was looking for fun, I shifted, which caused another sort of distraction.

"Look at the size of that lion's penis!"

"Imagine how much those furry balls would fetch on the black market," said another.

Everyone wanted to bag the trophy. If it wouldn't look dumb, I would have tucked my assets into some underpants; however, a mighty feline didn't wear clothes in his majestic state.

I did snarl as people kept trying to touch, though. I also almost chewed off the face of the guy who muttered, "Someone forgot to neuter their cat."

Touch my furry balls, asshole, and die.

A minute later, someone did die. By my paw, I must admit, mostly because I scented the witch on the fellow. Given she'd hung the miscreant on the railing, having magicked his clothes into rope, the dick deserved the swipe of my claws that sent him plummeting.

Good thing I'd signed the indemnity clause before boarding. What happened on the cruise stayed on the cruise.

My mother waylaid me next. "Ozzie, why aren't you upstairs with the others partying?"

In her fifties and looking trim for her age, my mom arched a brow as she waited for a reply. A good one too, or she'd order me back upstairs.

Shifting, I was ready with an excuse. "I was tired. Thought I'd hit the sack early."

"You can sleep in."

"Not if I want to hit the gym before breakfast."

"Since when are you that motivated in the morning?" Mom knew me so well. Then her expression went from suspicious to delighted. "Don't tell me you've already set your sights on a woman."

"You caught me." I shrugged and offered a sheepish smile. No need to tell her the woman wasn't mating material. My mother had a thing against witches.

"Who is she? Do I know her parents? Please don't tell me she's from that wolf pack on board. They're Canadian and won't shut up about their healthcare system. You know what,"—she waved a hand—"so what if she is. Fresh blood would do the pride some good."

"She's fresh, all right," I replied. As in not even compatible. Something about the way witches' magic wouldn't work on us also caused problems with the whole procreation bit. Add to that a feud that went back centuries…

"Here I am, getting in your way, making you late for your tryst." My mother shoved me. "Go. Have fun."

Don't mind if I do. I mean, a boy should never disobey his mother. Back on four feet, and getting tired of switching, I trotted after Glinda's enticing scent, only to get stopped. Again. This time by an old woman wearing a strapless dress patterned in a bold clash of flowers, hanging low due to her gravitationally-challenged cleavage.

"And where do you think you're going, giant feline?"

Another witch, I realized with a sniff. Her scent also hinted of the one I followed, making her most likely a family member. Perhaps she would help me.

I returned to my man shape, feeling fatigue tug at all the rapidly-spaced changes.

The older lady perused me and smacked her lips. "If I were a few centuries younger…"

Knowing full well how to play this game, I winked. "Experience is golden.

"Flirt." She smiled but wasn't distracted. "What are you doing in this part of the ship?"

"Taking a stroll," I offered her a shrug.

"There's nothing down this hall for you to see." She blocked me quite adeptly, especially since my mother had raised me to never lay a hand on a lady—or lose it. Happened to my cousin Horatio.

"Okay, you caught me." Said in my best aw-shucks tone. "I was checking on a witch. A relation of yours, I believe. Sister maybe?" I queried, earning a titter.

"Why are you stalking Jane?"

Jane? Such a simple name for a complex creature. "Just checking she made it to her room safely. She had an altercation with a pirate."

"Not even one day and she's having fun." The old lady beamed.

"She didn't seem very happy, so I thought I'd pay her a visit."

"I'm sure you did." Wink. "I can't believe my Janey has the boys chasing her already. Although, you're not what I would have expected." She eyed me again, and my hands dropped to cover my junk. "So, you found it then?"

"Found what?" I replied at a complete loss.

"The locket?"

"What locket?"

She frowned. "You don't have it?"

"Not a clue what you're talking about."

"Pity," she said with a sigh. "In that case, you shouldn't waste your time with my granddaughter." She sauntered past and said over her shoulder, "She's about to get engaged."

"To who?" I couldn't help but ask, annoyance with no basis filling me. The old lady didn't reply, and after she'd left, I stared at the door.

The door. Behind it was an interesting witch. One who was off-limits in more ways than one.

But that wasn't why I ended up getting royally drunk in my room.

See, when I'd asked the witch who Glinda was marrying, my inner feline muttered, *Us, you idiot.*

6

JANE: I'LL PUT HER IN A NICE HOME. THE KIND THAT GIVES THEM REAL JELL-O.

"I can't believe I lost track of my locket." I remained peeved as I paced my tiny coffin of a room. Grandma had really skimped on the accommodations. We had a pair of bunks and a miniscule washroom, that was it. Not enough room by far to properly pace and rant. A good thing my bag had a pocket dimension to hold everything I might need. Because right now, I needed a punching bag. And ice cream. Oh, and some whipped cream with cherries to go on top.

Except I'd forgotten to replenish my travel larder, and all I had to munch my annoyance away was stale black licorice.

Which was still delicious, if too chewy.

"This is all his fault." Not the pirate. That lion. How dare he get involved? How dare he be so hot?

How could I properly hate the man like I should when his abs had baby abs of their own? And then there was his feline, a sleek creature with a lush, dark mane. He stood out compared to the golden-hued lions I'd seen before.

But forget about him.

"I need to find that locket." Pronto. Before the wrong sort ended up in possession of it. What if I accidentally fell in love with a ghoul? Or, the dark lord forbid, a shifter?

I'd never hear the end of it at family reunions. Just look at Great-Aunt Leona, who married that wolf that worked on Wall Street. Everyone whispered about how disgustingly rich she was, and how many well-behaved children she had, and the lovely house she owned in the snooty part of town...

Hmmm. On second thought, that didn't help the case.

Besides, I panicked for nothing. Magic didn't work on shifters. Which meant my locket would never end up in the paws of one. I hoped. With my luck, love spells would be the one exception to the rule.

"Where are you, Grandma?" Who knew where she had gotten to? For all I knew, she'd planted the locket on the pirate herself. A poor choice if you asked me. Did she really think I wanted to date my father?

Gross.

Almost as bad as that shifter who'd gotten in my way. No surprise that my thoughts turned back to Oz. But with good cause. He was the reason I didn't have my necklace. What had possessed him to chase that pirate in the first place?

And did he have no shame? Standing around afterward, naked as the day he was born, his big, bulky body on display. Then there was that massive erection.

So massive.

For me.

That tingly feeling between my legs happened again. I immediately squelched it. Witches might not have many standards, but in my family, we did at least know better than to consort with Oz's kind. Grandma tended to be old school in that respect. I still remembered her cackling in glee as her nemesis, Rasputin, had a granddaughter who married some feline. Which wasn't enough to stem her jealousy when the other granddaughter of her enemy married the Antichrist.

Personally, I was jealous of the fact that this Evangeline character, the one with the pussy husband, got the title *Wickedest Witch* when all I got from my peers was the Bitchy Witch. Also well deserved, but not as cool.

If I cared about such things. Which I didn't. What

I cared about was getting my damned locket back—without a husband attached to it.

If the pirate no longer had it, then who did? All I knew for sure was that it remained somewhere on the ship. I could feel the faint link between it and me, but I was too tired to deal with it tonight. Especially since wandering the ship meant dealing with drunken ogres, centaurs, and other creatures. Best wait until morning when the night owls and sun-challenged were all passed out.

I cast a spell so I could sleep. The following day, I readied myself to face the world. It took a few stabs in the bag before I located some clothes and made it to breakfast. I'd concocted a dull plan, which consisted of wandering around the ship until the locket tugged at me. With no clear place to start my search, I began in the dining room, which was set up with tables in rounds and a massive buffet.

The room was emptier than expected. People, demons, things sleeping off their hangovers. The lack of a crowd made it easy for Grandma to spot me.

"There's my sweet granddaughter," she exclaimed, her voice almost as bright as her ensemble, an orange blouse tucked into a green skirt. But most astonishing of all…

"Grandma, where are your wrinkles?" I demanded. Because the woman in front of me, while definitely the one who'd spent a good portion of my life raising me, looked nothing like the matron who'd arrived on the boat. Now sporting an age of around forty, her face had smoothed, her boobs had lifted, and she'd even shaved her legs! Longer appendages than she'd had when we landed on the ship.

"Please, you didn't actually think a witch of my powers looks that old, did you?" Grandma snickered. "I only wear an age glamour to keep the mundanes in the neighborhood from noticing."

"But…but…" I had no words to explain the annoyance with myself that I'd never caught on. In my defense, the house was steeped in magic, and thus, I always assumed the miasma of power around Grandma was natural.

"Close your mouth, dear. We don't want people to think you're easy, now do we?" She used a fingertip to shut my jaw.

Speaking of easy… "Where were you last night?" I said, crossing my arms. "You didn't sleep in your bed."

"None of your business. But if it makes you feel better, I don't think I got pregnant."

I almost choked. Then I did cough as a deep voice behind me said, "Morning, Glinda."

"You!" I whirled and glared at Oz, who had the temerity to wear a grin—and clothing. Jerk.

"You again? Why, a lady might start thinking you're stalking her and welcome it?" Grandma tossed her head.

The comment had me eyeing my grandma. "You know this man?"

"Not well enough yet," she purred.

Gag.

"Any time you want to have a chat…" Oz flirted right back.

"Hands off the pussy," I snapped to Grandma. "And you keep your dirty paws off my grandmother."

"Does this mean I should keep my pawing to you?" he riposted.

"Don't make me find a leash," I growled.

Whereas Grandma beamed. "Well, good for you, finally claiming yourself a pet."

Oz choked with laughter, whereas I gritted my teeth. "He's not my anything."

"Then that makes him fair game." Grandma eyed Oz up and down and might have said more if a voice didn't interrupt. "Good morning, Dottie." The demi-demon from the day before appeared with a big smile.

"Who's Dottie?" I asked.

Grandma pursed her lips. "Me."

I frowned. "Since when?" Grandma was just… Grandma. Unless she was hanging with her friends, who called her Dorothy.

"She's been Dottie for a long time. She used to hate her real name, seeing as how she got it before that Baum fellow made it famous," Shax advised with a wink. Then, to my grandma, he said, "So delighted you are joining me for breakfast."

"You wish," she scoffed. "I am eating with Jane."

"Ah, yes, your lovely granddaughter." Shax sketched me a bow. "So nice to see you again."

"Not really," grumbled my grandma, and I finally knew how to get back at her.

"You know what? You really should have breakfast with Shax. Catch up on old times."

"I have nothing to say to him." Grandma tilted her chin.

"Just as stubborn as ever."

"Must be a family trait," muttered Oz, which earned him a jab and a glare from me.

"It is too early for this. I need a mimosa," muttered Grandma before she stomped off. With a demi-demon shadow.

"I wonder who he is," I muttered aloud. I'd never seen Grandma let anyone get under her skin before.

"I thought you knew his name." Oz had yet to disappear.

"I do. Shax something or other." I shrugged.

Oz snapped his fingers. "I know that name. Uncle to the captain from what I heard," said Oz, who remained by my side. Fully clothed. Annoying me. Mostly because I'd prefer he wore nothing at all.

"Don't you have some mice to chase for breakfast?" I asked.

"I prefer honey drizzled on succulent fruit." His gaze was on my mouth. His words stroked me with phantom fingers. My libido woke up, starved for more.

"Must you make everything about sex?"

He angled a brow. "I don't know what you mean."

Was it me and my horny girly bits turning innocuous words into something dirty? "I need coffee."

"As my witch commands." He snared a cup from a passing waiter and held it out, waiting until it was filled to the brim before handing it to me.

"Who says I drink it black?"

He smiled. "You want cream, just say the word."

I choked down a scalding mouthful. While my tongue tried to recover from the abuse, I veered my attention to the entrance of our illustrious captain. Adexios, son of the infamous Charon, the boatman for the Styx. Which wasn't as reassuring as you'd think. Even on the mundane side, everyone had heard about Adexios's mishaps. He'd lost more souls in the crossings than all the other boatmen combined.

"How was the rest of your evening once we parted ways?" Oz asked.

Boring. Lonely. Sans batteries because, apparently, I'd forgotten to pack some. "Fine." Then I don't know where the urge to be polite came from, but I said, "Yours?"

"Lonely. Boring. Lacking the company of a lady."

"Did your inflatable doll pop under your claws?" Spoken with a sweet smile.

The laughter that burst from him caught me off guard and warmed me.

"You're clever," he said. Not gorgeous. Or entrancing.

Clever. A compliment I actually appreciated.

"I see you found your pants." Words I regretted the moment they left my lips.

"Just say the word, and I'll lose them again." He winked.

A wink shouldn't have the ability to make my girly parts clench with giddiness. "How about you stay away from me?"

"Be nice, Glinda. After all, you're going to thank me in a minute."

"Doubtful." I inched away from him, aiming for the chocolate croissants that suddenly caught my eye. Almost as good as sex. Surely, they'd help with my current problem.

Alas, sex on two legs followed. "You are trying to find something on this ship, and I want to help you."

Suddenly suspicious, I eyed him. "Why would you do that? You barely know me."

"I know enough."

"You don't like me," I stated baldly.

"I wouldn't say that. You're interesting."

"So the offer of aid is because of a cat's curiosity fetish?" And not because I was irresistible. Good, because I didn't want him to like me.

"My feline interest in you is only part of it. By spending time hunting down what you lost, I get to avoid my family."

I gaped at him. "You've got family here? You cad!" I shoved at him. "What is wrong with you?"

Oz allowed me to shove him—not that he budged—and chuckled. "I didn't abandon my wife and kids if that's what you're thinking. I'm single since you seem interested. I was talking about my parents and sisters. Plus, some cousins. Aunts. Uncles. You know…*family*."

Embarrassment heated my cheeks, followed by a strange relief. "Why do you want to avoid them? I thought cats were all about family gatherings."

He grimaced. "My sister is getting married. Which means tons of giggling, a hopeful mother of the bride eyeing her only son, and handsy bridesmaids. Trust me when I say I'd rather stick close to you than deal with them."

"You do realize if any of them comes near me, I'm liable to say something nasty."

His grin widened. "I'm counting on it. Now, move aside. If I'm going to play the part of tracker, I need some of those pastries."

"I never agreed."

"Say yes."

For a moment, I floundered, my mind flashing to every stupid, sappy, romantic movie I'd ever seen. Except Oz wasn't proposing marriage to me. "I shouldn't."

"Scared of a pussy cat?"

There was something about being challenged that made an idiot out of people. "Fine. You want to help, then go right ahead."

He took my acceptance to mean he could lean past me and snare five croissants to my one. Plus a heaping platter of bacon. Then Oz handed me a tray of sausage.

"I don't want any," I managed to say.

"But you do have a free hand."

And he just went right ahead and used it. Kind of taken by surprise, I allowed it. Shocking, I know, but what can I say? The idea of using his nose to help me find my locket intrigued. It had nothing at all to do with the fact that being close to him made me all tingly inside.

He led. I followed. Don't judge. What could I say? He might be an animal, but he had a nice ass in tight jeans. Not the usual attire for the tropics, but it worked for him.

Oz led us right to the captain's table, and I might have groaned except young Grandma was there, doing her best to ignore the demi-demon sitting beside her. A handsome demon I should add, with silver wings in his dark hair from which poked a pair of ebony horns, a swarthy complexion, and a way of making my grandma silent that I'd give anything to learn.

I went to sit down across from them when a tiny voice squeaked, "Don't squish me."

A glance down showed a child-sized body in a robe, perched in the chair I'd have sworn was empty.

"Sorry."

"Don't apologize," a stern voice said. A turn of my head showed the captain speaking. "Someone's been playing with his invisibility again. What did I tell you about messing with our guests?"

The little voice piped, "That was Cory you told that to. You only told me no feeding the passengers to the sea monsters. Which is so unfair. They're hungry."

"Kelly." A warning tone emerged with the name. "You know you're supposed to be at your lessons."

"I hate school. I'd rather be fighting," grumbled the tyke. "You're no fun. I'm going to see Mum." The little robed figure disappeared.

The captain sighed. "Children…I think I'm beginning to understand why my parents only had one. Good Morning, Miss Davey. And you must be Ozmodeus Alexopolous. Won't you join us?"

"Ozmodeus," I snickered.

He leaned close enough to whisper in my ear. "You can keep using Oz. Easier to scream when you come."

The very idea had me clenching and aroused. So very, very turned on.

I felt up the seat before gingerly taking my place, and Oz helped tuck in my chair, which caused me a second of surprise. Since when did that happen? Chivalry had died right around the time women started showing their ankles, at least according to Grandma.

While I could tuck in my own chair, I had to say there was something courtly in the fact that Oz did it automatically.

He took the spot beside me, and given the size of the seat versus the width of him, his leg pressed against mine. Hard to ignore. But I did my best. Part of my strategy involved keeping my gaze firmly on the captain.

Adexios of no last name that I'd discovered, looked nothing like Charon…then again, no one knew what the boatman looked like. Charon was only ever seen in robes swathing every bit of his features. His son, though, wore a white uniform adorned with gold braid at the shoulders. A hat sat on the table beside his cutlery. A handsome enough guy, I supposed, but married with kids. Which put him off-limits.

Not that I was looking for candidates, but the spell would. That locket could be anywhere. I had to keep my guard up.

"I hear we're making port shortly," I said to start a conversation.

"Not exactly," Adexios explained. "We're going to drop anchor in Mermaid Bay and lower the floating docks so guests can go for a swim."

"I thought mermaids were dangerous." My father used to tell me stories about the mermaids dragging his crew off the ship and drowning them in the deep.

"Not this particular group. They've interbred with humans enough that they're quite tame compared to their counterparts in Hell."

"I don't swim," the lion beside me declared.

"No doubt. Probably don't want to get that silky

mane soggy," I said, taking a dainty bite of my croissant.

"I don't mind getting my hair wet. For the right reasons." His gaze dipped to my lap.

My cheeks burned, and the bite of pastry got stuck. I took a gulp of coffee.

"If you don't go for a dip, then you won't get to see Jane in a bikini," declared my grandma.

I glared. "I don't have a bikini."

"If you forgot to shave, I know a spell," she offered.

Before I could die of mortification, Oz chimed in. "Nothing lovelier than a lady au natural."

"We have an entire section in the library devoted to poetry on a female's bush." Said by Shax as if it were a serious subject.

I gaped. "Poetry?"

Grandma snorted. "You should ask him how large the section of limericks about male prowess is."

At the dig, Shax grinned. "Still under construction as we keep adding new ones daily."

"You work in a library?" I asked.

"Used to. I retired."

"Doubtful," Grandma muttered. "I remember how much you loved your damned books."

"I've changed."

"Hmmph."

I found this exchange fascinating. There was obviously history between the two.

"Did you guys used to date?" I asked.

"No."

"Yes."

I blinked. "Which one is it?"

"Shax was too busy with his job at the library to date."

He pursed his lips. "More like too shy. And then you were a little too married."

"She's single now," I offered.

"I know." Shax bestowed a look upon Grandma that she did her best to ignore. Unfortunately, she caught the attention of someone else.

Gaston, the pirate, looking as disreputable as before, slid into the chair beside my grandma. "Hello there, my lovely."

"Hello to you, too," she purred, batting her lashes.

What was happening here?

It set Shax to scowling and Gaston to leering. "After breakfast, care to swab my deck?" The wink left nothing to the imagination.

And Grandma didn't slap him.

"Excuse me!" I exclaimed. "That's my grandma you're talking dirty to." I snapped my fingers, and Gaston grimaced as bubbles frothed from his lips. "As for you…" I narrowed my gaze on my grandmother. "Don't make me recreate that spell that will put you in menopause again."

"I'm a grown woman, Jane." Grandma stood and threw her napkin on the table. "You can't tell me what to do."

"You heard the lady, she— Arrgh." The pirate's chair tipped over, Shax appeared smug, and I just scowled.

"I should have stayed in my room."

Beside me, Oz snickered. "But then breakfast wouldn't have been half as entertaining."

That earned him a stomp on the toes under the table.

The jerk didn't even wince. Oz did, however, reach for my hand under the tablecloth.

Why? Why was he holding my hand? I stared at our fingers intertwined.

Thankfully, distraction came from a new direction. "I insist on talking to him." The strident tone broke through the hum of conversation.

"Oh, shit," muttered Oz. He released my hand as a beautiful woman stalked over to our table and began shrieking at Adexios, something about flowers.

Oz did his best to unobtrusively slide into the next seat over, leaving a gap between us.

It shouldn't have hurt. I should have ignored it. Instead, I steamed.

I glared at him. "Cad."

"It's not what you think."

I knew what I thought. The gorgeous woman haranguing the captain over wedding preparations must be Oz's sister. "You're embarrassed to be seen with me," I hissed. The humiliation burned hot.

"Am not."

I only had to flick my gaze at the empty seat between us for his jaw to tighten. "Trust me when I say you don't want to be caught on my sister's radar."

"Ozzie!" The bride-to-be turned from the dazed captain to her brother. "Where have you been hiding? I haven't seen you since dinner last night."

Perhaps it was the bitch in me, or maybe I wanted to impress my lord, the devil, but I was the one to reply for Oz. "He was with me."

"You?" Such disbelief in the one word as the woman eyed me up and down. Then laughed. "Ozzie. Come." She snapped her fingers.

I made the sound of a whip, and while everyone watched to see what he would do, Oz sighed.

"Really, Jellia. We talked about this. I am not your little harem boy to scurry at your whim."

"You're my brother, and it's my wedding." Her lower lip stuck out in a pout.

"I'm here. Isn't that enough?"

Judging by the storm brewing on his sister's face? No.

"Don't be a wet pussy. Show your sis some love," I

mocked.

"Love? Gross. Nasty. What's love got to do with anything? Don't tell me you invited my boring brother to this cruise." One didn't need the whiff of brimstone to know who'd arrived.

Lucifer, looking younger than I recalled, appeared in a puff of smoke, wearing a blue blazer, a white ascot, a jauntily tilted cap, and flip-flops etched in jellyfish. On anyone else, it might have seemed ridiculous, but the devil knew how to carry off the fashion faux pas with panache.

"My dark lord, you honor us with your presence." Grandma gave him a small curtsy.

"What can I say? I am the best devil I can be. When I don't have to deal with my brother. Where is he?" Lucifer spun his head around for a peek.

"I did not invite your brother," Adexios mumbled. "You know Charlie still has him grounded for getting that woman pregnant and then locking her up in that dark dimension."

"Who knew he'd one day make me so proud." Lucifer put a hand to his chest. "You know that's twice now he's impregnated a woman and tried to not take responsibility. I, on the other hand, proudly claim all my bastards."

"Speaking of which, congrats on your new son." My grandma didn't miss an opportunity to kiss the dark lord's ass.

"Ah, yes, the bane of my existence, the impending tool of my doom. The Antichrist is thriving probably because he gets exclusive use of my wife's tits. Unfair, I tell you. Those beautiful, firm apples are mine." Lucifer mimed palming a pair and licked his lips. "But I mustn't think of them. I must be strong, apparently, until they are mine again!" The evil chuckle vibrated, and no one spoke. It ended with the devil rubbing his hands. "Someone point me in the direction of the mimosas and bikinis."

Thunder cracked outside, and Lucifer glared overhead. "Just because we're married, wench doesn't mean I can't look."

A crack of lightning followed by a deep rumbling thunder said otherwise. The joys of Lucifer being married to Mother Earth. He never got away with anything anymore.

The devil's gaze alighted on me, the slitted eyes narrowed, and his grin widened. "Why, if it isn't my own bitchy witch." I didn't know if I should be flattered or annoyed that he knew me by my nickname.

"Dark Lord, you grace me with your presence." I didn't feel a need to curtsy or bow. After all, he'd seen me dancing naked in his name.

"I can't wait for tonight," he said with a wink. Which caused more thunder to rattle the windows in the dining room. Lucifer rolled his eyes all around his head, which proved to be disturbing. "Oh, stop the drama, wench. You know I won't be touching them. I'm saving all that horny power for when I defile you after."

Oz nudged me as he leaned close to whisper. "What's tonight?"

"Summer solstice and a full moon." I didn't say anything more, mostly because Lucifer fixed us with a calculating gaze.

"Why, what do my eyes see but a witch and a lion, getting cozy. Find a wardrobe, and this could get interesting."

"Don't you start your matchmaking shenanigans with my granddaughter," my grandma—who was looking more and more like my aunt with her new face—interjected.

"Me? Encourage the course of true love?" The devil couldn't sound innocent if he tried.

"More like shoving," coughed Adexios.

That drew Lucifer's attention. "Are you complaining?"

"Heck, no," exclaimed the captain. "If it weren't for your shoving, I'd have never met Valaska."

"And people said I didn't know what I was doing." Lucifer patted himself on the back with a pair of arms that appeared out of nowhere.

"Well, there was that demoness that killed the five suitors you tried to set her up with," the demi-demon by my grandma's side reminded.

"Not my fault," grumbled the devil. "She should have said something sooner about preferring dryads."

"And the captain in your legion who cut off his own arm rather than stay with that ghouless?" Shax apparently had an arsenal of examples.

"Turned out he'd said he liked a woman who could cook a mean gruel, not a ghoul. I'm not perfect. Far from it." Lucifer winked and managed to make it seem utterly lascivious.

"No messing with my passengers," Adexios warned. "This is not the Love Boat."

"Gag me with a giant tit, I should hope not," the devil gasped. "I'd like to see a little violence, blood, maybe a few flying limbs. It wouldn't be a cruise without some shenanigans."

Oz snickered.

"Did you say something, pussy cat?" Lucifer's head spun a full one-eighty.

"Nope. Not me." The kitty grinned. "And just so you know, I'll be doing my part to earn my place in your kingdom when I die."

Because no one wanted to go to Heaven. It was said the souls up there tended to commit crimes out of boredom just to escape. Although, with Charlie now in charge, things might get more interesting...

"Waaaaaaa!" The strident yodel of a baby caused the devil to wince.

"Dammit. He woke already. Why won't that child sleep?" Lucifer shook his fist before poofing out of sight.

"So it's true he had a son?" Oz asked.

"Yes, although there is discussion as to whether or not Damian is truly the Antichrist. Because in the legends, nothing ever said the Son of Perdition would be born *in* wedlock. It's put the scholars in quite a tizzy," Shax explained.

"How do you know that?" I asked.

"I told you, Shax is a librarian." Grandmother sneered. "Loves his books more than anything else." And with that statement, she stood, dumped her juice on the demon's head, and walked out.

Rather than appear angry, the man smiled. "I think she's softening," Shax claimed before taking his leave.

The captain went next, declaring that he needed to pretend to actually steer the ship but, rest assured, he wouldn't actually be touching anything. The real sailors would be handling the navigation.

Even Oz's sister had left, fleeing around the time Lucifer had arrived, leaving me alone with Oz and a quiet woman at the far end of the table who kept staring at the ring on her finger rather than conversing.

"When should we start looking?" Oz asked, pushing aside his now-empty plates.

"How about now?" The sooner we found the locket, the quicker I could get rid of the kitty who shivered me timbers.

Ack. Being at sea had me channeling my dad. Next thing you knew, I'd be trying to strip the guests of their jewels and ravaging the men. A.k.a, Oz.

"We can start as soon as I get a fix on the scent."

"How can you do that when I don't have the item?"

"It's keyed to you, isn't it?" he asked.

"Yes."

"Then just stand close to me so I can get a sense for you."

"How close?"

He dragged me from my chair into his lap. I stiffened. So did he. In one spot.

"Is this an excuse to grope me?"

"I don't need an excuse, Glinda." His arms draped around me, and his face nuzzled against my neck, my ear, my hair.

I did my best to not tremble in his grasp. *Please don't let him know how much his presence affects me.* My mind did its best to deny the knowledge that he could probably smell my arousal.

"Are you done yet?"

Oz moved under me, his erection evident, which in turn made me wet. He growled softly against me, the vibration of it on my skin making me shiver.

How much longer would this take?

His hand stroked up and down my back. The heat of his breath was in my hair. The spot between my legs pulsed with need.

Crazy need.

He stood abruptly, dumping me from his lap, not that he let me fall. He held on to me, his big hands on my waist, holding me steady.

A good thing, too, because my knees were malfunctioning. I glanced up at Oz and saw his eyes glowing. Gold and intent.

I swallowed. "Did you get what you needed?"

"Not quite." He reeled me closer. "I just have to—"

The ship shuddered as it came to a stop, and the intercom announced, "We've arrived at Mermaid Bay. Participating guests should gather on the lower deck for a swim."

A great cue for me to step away from the much-too-sexy Oz.

He grumbled, "Where are you going?"

"To put on my bathing suit." Because that tugging feeling was back in my chest, and it let me know I'd be getting wet.

Or at least wetter. My poor panties didn't survive my proximity to Oz, and I could feel his stare on my backside as I hurried away.

But did he sense my disappointment when he didn't follow?

7

OZ: I FINALLY UNDERSTAND THE EXPRESSION, I CAN'T ALWAYS GET WHAT I WANT. BUT WHAT IF I NEED...?

IT TOOK CLENCHING my fists and rooting my feet to keep me from following Jane. My lack of action made my inner feline yowl.

Why aren't you chasing her?

The scent of her lingered, making me hard. So fucking hard. And yet I couldn't forget my conversation with the old woman last night—a witch who had turned into a younger one today.

She's about to get engaged. And it only took a bottle of rum to figure out that the locket Jane's grandma had spoken of, and the thing that Jane sought were one and the same. A necklace possessed by Jane's future husband. No wonder she was so eager to find it.

So was I, and I couldn't figure out why. If I wanted to rid myself of the witch, I simply had to stay out of her way. Hang with my family. Lock myself in my room. Yet, instead, I'd drunk a vile concoction to handle my hangover and made sure to locate her first thing this morning.

Then tortured myself by holding her hand. What kind of dork did that? The same one that used the lamest excuse in the world to get her sitting in my lap. Feeling her. Smelling her.

Wanting her.

Must have her.

Oh, hell no. Witches and shifters didn't mix. Often, I should add. There were issues with the whole compatibility thing—the creation of babies requiring special intervention—not to mention the stigma from friends and family. Which I never understood. Nothing wrong with Jane, and it wasn't as if she could use magic to harm me.

Why am I looking for excuses? Because that's what I was doing. The realization brought a sigh.

So, what next?

I'd promised to help her. And I would. Right after I ditched my sister again.

Witnessing her confrontation with the captain at breakfast had only convinced me that I needed to stay far away from all things wedding. One more day and this horror show would be over.

Since I now had a good sense of what I was looking for, it didn't prove too hard to find a hint of magic that reminded me of Jane. The faint trail led me to the lower deck where people were being floated down by ship staff or descending ladders to floating platforms. The scent ended at the railing, and I could only glance out over the many bobbing heads. Who among them had the locket?

My gaze passed over the eager crowd and then returned to one particular shape. She might be wrapped in a towel, but despite only knowing Jane one day, I recognized the stance.

My witch.

Er. The witch.

Fuck.

She stood beside the slim form of the same woman who'd been so quiet at breakfast and dropped the towel.

I greedily inhaled the sight of Jane. She wasn't wearing a bikini at all—leading to some disappointment—but I did enjoy the view of her in the one-piece swimsuit with a sheer, black cover-up. She stared into the water, making me wonder if she'd seen someone jump in with the locket.

"Hey, handsome," a voice gurgled from below. I looked down to see a bobbing face with streaming green hair.

"Taken," I replied without even thinking.

"Lucky lady." With a flip of her tail, the mermaid was gone, and yet I stared a moment longer as I tried to figure out why my mouth betrayed me.

I was most certainly not taken. Not even dating. Or interested. Nothing.

All things I reassured myself with, even as I turned my attention back to Jane. She'd slipped off her sheer robe and stood on the edge of the platform, her shape tempting me with the indent of her waist, and the subtle flair of her hips. With Jane's hair pulled back into a tight bun, the smooth column of her neck teased. How nice would it look with a set of teeth marks?

I blinked and shook my head.

What is wrong with me?

A disturbance beneath the surface stirred the water beside the dock. A tentacle emerged from below. The young woman from breakfast, Sasha something or other, screamed and darted behind Jane.

I wasn't worried. Magic would subdue any threat. Only Jane didn't act, which meant she ended up curled in the sea monster's grasp and dragged into the water!

Oh, hell no.

A roar emerged as I vaulted the rail, choosing to keep my man shape as I angled into a dive and sluiced into the warm water. It took me a moment to orient myself, the clear depths a chaotic swirl of bodies jumping in, jewel-colored tails flashing, and seaweed hair floating. But none of that interested me.

I surfaced for a moment, only to grab a deep lungful of air and resubmerge myself. I kicked and pulled with my arms, aiming for the deep. Too far ahead of me, I could see the witch being dragged down, her mouth clamped tight, her expression full of annoyance. She couldn't waggle her fingers with her arms pinned by her sides.

She needed me. So, I swam as hard as I could. The moment she saw me, her eyes widened. But not in appreciation. She shook her head, and I didn't grasp the warning until the tentacle knocked me head over ass, and unconscious.

8

JANE: THAT WASN'T A KISS.

The idiot came to save me. Dove into the water despite declaring earlier that he couldn't swim. Not entirely true, he did some pathetic cat crawl trying to reach me.

Yes, me. Then the jerk got himself knocked senseless and started to sink. All those muscles weighed him down.

The lion required a rescue, which meant the sea monster with my locket would have to wait.

Yes, my locket. As soon as that tentacle came whipping from the water, I'd seen the golden glint of my precious. Hence why I didn't fight as the appendage curled around me and dragged me into the ocean. Having been raised around water, I'd sucked in a deep breath, and took the first few moments to catch my bearings while trying to locate where my necklace had gone.

It appeared stuck on one of the sea monster's suckers and dangled just out of reach. I had to be careful. If I killed the beast and it sank, I'd lose the locket. Not entirely a bad thing, given the spell on it; however, I wanted the memento from my mother.

Before I could act, Oz interfered once more. The idiot did some pathetic dive into the water and then did his strange sea-scrabble to try and reach me.

It was stupid.

And cute.

Sweet enough that I couldn't let him drown. I wiggled my toes and pulled at my magic. Which some might mistakenly assume weak given I was underwater. That only applied to regular witches. Not only was I descended from a long line of sea witches, I was half pirate, too. The ocean sang in my blood.

The jolt of magic I expelled forced the tentacle to release me, and I wasted no time. Hands by my sides, I shoved out more magic to propel my body to the sinking man.

Oz's eyes were closed, his body limp. There was no reaction when I snared a hold of his shirt. A garment that couldn't hold the body. He slipped out of it, and I had to go deeper, my lungs starting to protest. I grabbed

Oz more firmly this time, my arms around his torso, expelling magic through my toes. A little more erratic when it came to guiding us, yet we emerged with a splash and a flop, like a submarine suddenly surfacing.

I sucked in a huge breath, but he didn't. I quickly stroked to a floating dock where cruise line employees stood by and helped to heave Oz from the water. They turned him onto his side and acted in his best interest.

I didn't care. I shoved them aside.

"Let me handle this." I knelt by him and put my hands on his chest, willing my magic into his lungs, drawing out the seawater in them. It emerged in wet gouts, and still, he didn't breathe.

"Come on, Oz. Don't you dare die. You haven't found my locket yet," I grumbled even as I didn't understand my concern for him.

I pressed on his chest, applying compression, and when that still didn't work, I leaned down to put my lips on his. A breath into his mouth. Stop. Breathe in. Stop.

At the same time, I willed him to live. *Come on, kitty. You don't want to die yet.*

I straddled him, and that was the only reason I noticed him recovering. The cock pinned under me swelled. The soft lips I'd been breathing past hardened, and the lifesaving turned into kissing.

Oz woke suddenly—horny—flipping me onto my

back, the hardness of him pressing against me, his lips slanting over mine and taking over the embrace, igniting my senses.

It took the crowd cheering us on, "Live porno! Someone get a camera," for me to realize that we had an audience—and almost not care.

Grandma, on the other hand, cared. She screeched, "Not again! Get that animal off my granddaughter. She's supposed to be engaged to someone else."

No, I wasn't. Screw the current owner of the locket. Like hell was I marrying a sea monster.

But the kiss had to end. Mostly because someone yanked on Oz, exclaiming, "What are you doing? Mom and Jellia will kill you if they see you making out with a witch."

The fact that Oz roared his displeasure helped. That he rolled off me annoyed.

I went to sit up and found myself smothered in a towel with Grandma screeching, "Have some respect for yourself, Janey. Don't be your mother."

Sigh.

For a moment, I'd forgotten who he was, where I was, and what I wanted. Which was to not be involved with any man.

As I got to my feet, my gaze met Oz's for a moment as he looked away from his haranguing sibling. Our eyes locked. Heat and awareness passed through the gaze. A whisper with no voice that said—

The strange connection between us broke as something whipped from the water, spraying water droplets and causing the crowd on the floating dock to utter an "Ooooh."

The tentacle from the deep was back. Unlike mundane humans, the milling passengers didn't run screaming and blubbering in fear. Rather, excitement tinged the air as a few waved their arms and shouted, "Me next! Me! Me!"

Because nothing screamed fun on a cruise like being dragged to a drowning death by a sea monster.

The blubbery-skinned thing with the suction pads held my locket, the gold exterior of it glinting in the sun. Even as I stared, the amulet went soaring into the air, arcing high overhead to land somewhere on the ship.

Looking for a new suitor.

And it wasn't the wet lion shaking his mane all over the deck.

9

OZ: I WILL NOT TOSS MY SISTER OVERBOARD.

My sister, Jinjur, disappeared as I was still wringing the nasty seawater from my long, luscious locks. I was delaying the inevitable. Someone, likely Jinjur, was sure to tattle about my swim. Which meant…

"Ozzie!" The shrill use of my nickname made me cringe. Yet there was nowhere to hide, not unless I planned to go for another dip, and I'd had enough of the water for today. Although, I did have a hankering for seafood.

"Hey, Jellia." I gave my sister my best smile. It did nothing to dispel her mighty scowl.

"Don't you *hi* me. I know what you've been up to. Ditching the wedding festivities to go—"

I interrupted. "For a refreshing dip. You should try it. The water is quite warm."

A remark overheard by a guest who felt a need to explain why. "Mermaid pee."

The very idea had me determined to grab a shower. Pity I couldn't shake my sister. The harangue continued even once I reached my suite.

"What is wrong with you?"

"Not much. I'm pretty perfect, as a matter of fact." Modesty was for wolves.

"Really, Ozzie. People saw you consorting with a witch. In public. While sober."

"Shouldn't we be more concerned about Jinjur's quickness to snitch?" Ratted out by my baby sister, and within minutes of the kiss no less. Which made me wonder if Jane had suffered the same dressing-down by her grandmother. Family might mean well, but sometimes, they should really just mind their own fucking business.

"Is *she* the reason you ditched the family fun arts and crafts hour?"

"Can you blame me? Glue and fur do not mix," I grumbled.

"Neither do lions and witches."

"Not entirely true."

"Don't you dare use that fictional story as evidence. We don't have a wardrobe or a magical land. And you are not Aslan." My sister, shatterer of boyhood fantasies.

"Maybe not, but I am a man, and I don't do crafts."

"Because you'd rather go swimming with *her*." Hissed with feline disdain.

"She's nice if you'd get to know her." Not entirely true. Jane tended to be acerbic, but her tongue in my mouth had been divine. Sweet and salty. My favorite.

"I don't have time to get to know her. My wedding is tonight. As in hours from now. *Hours*, Ozzie. I don't have time to deal with your midlife crisis and this sudden fetish for a witch. You should be worrying about me!" My sister looked so sweet and docile on the outside, barely reaching my chin. Yet inside that tiny body was a full-on she-cat in bridezilla mode.

"Everything will be perfect." I did my job as her brother to reassure. Meanwhile, I had no idea of the true status of the event. My experience with weddings was to show up when told, and dance with a few older aunts.

"It had better be perfect, or else." Which, coming from Jellia, did cause concern. She could retaliate like no one's business.

"My baby sister is getting married. What could possibly go wrong?" I tried a reassuring smile, and it almost got smacked off.

"I hate you. You have no idea of the stress I'm under."

Didn't she mean the stress she put the wedding planners under? My sister proved to be the grand 'zilla of brides.

"How is the wedding prep going?" As she'd made sure to remind me, my sister was getting married tonight, just before the full moon. Then she planned to party by the light of it. While she plotted how to terrorize her future husband, the rest of the wedding guests would be getting drunk and having sex with random strangers. The usual at a wedding. Nine months from now, there'd be plenty of surprise babies.

"How's it going?" she practically shrieked. "Like poop melting in the hot sun. Melinda,"—a bridesmaid—"got a sunburn. But not just any sunburn. She looks like a goddamned raccoon. Loretta is seasick and has managed to puke on everyone at this point. Ginny lost her shoes and only has flip-flops to wear because no one else is a size fourteen. And Patsy's hair turned orange from the gelatin pool she swam in."

None of which seemed urgent to me, but judging by my sister's expression, it might cause the end of the world. "Shit, that's a bummer." The right reply that got me a tirade about how stressed out she was, blah blah blah. I nodded at the appropriate times.

"You should relax. Have a drink." Maybe a pitcher of them.

"Relax?" Jellia snorted. "Yeah, okay. Sure. I'm surprised you're so calm, considering."

"What's that supposed to mean?"

"Mom."

One word to bring dread to my poor gut. "What about Mom?"

"She knows about the witch."

"How? Who told her?" Did I have time to hide? Because the bride having a fit was nothing compared to Mama Lion getting her claws in a snit.

"Who do you think?" My sister's smirk made me cringe.

I peered around my suite as if I expected my mother to pounce. "What did she say?" Laugh all you want, but my mother is not someone you messed with.

"Nothing."

"Uh-oh." Growing up, we'd learned that Mother keeping it in ended up being worse than her freaking out.

"It's your own fault, you know." My sister lacked sympathy for my dire dilemma. "You should have stayed away."

"I can't." The truth slipped out.

"What is it about the witch that has you acting like you rolled in a field of catnip? I've never seen you act so irrationally and it's not like she can spell you." Witch and warlock magic tended to break if it touched shifters. "So, what gives?"

Explain how Jane fascinated me? How having her around meant a constant boner? In many respects, Jellia was right. Jane was a drug to me. "It's not what you think."

"Are you, or are you not, fucking her?" Blunt, but that was my sister.

"Not." I didn't add the *yet* part.

"But you're obviously trying to get in her pants."

Well, duh. I was a guy, after all. But I might as well gut myself before admitting that to my sister. "She needs my help with something."

"Funny, because it looked more like she helped you."

An embarrassing reminder that Jane had saved me from drowning. I'd have to do something gloriously masculine and stupid to make up for it. "She lost something. I'm tracking it for her."

"Let me guess, she lost her panties, and you're going up her skirt to see if you can find them." Jellia rolled her eyes.

Worst part? She wasn't entirely wrong. I did want to get closer to Jane. But since I valued the lives I had left, I would never admit it. "Since you're so nosy, I'm helping the witch look for a locket. She lost it on the ship."

"A locket?" Jellia's brows rose. "It's kind of weird

you mention that, because on my way to find you, there was this dude on deck, just chilling, and out of nowhere, this necklace came flying and just about clocked him."

"You saw the locket?" My jaw might have dropped at the news.

"I don't know if it was *the* locket. But, yeah, he caught the necklace. And I swear, it was like the act shook him. He literally shuddered."

"Who is he? What does he look like?" I couldn't help but blurt it out, jealousy suddenly burning hot inside me.

"No idea. But he's cute as shit. If I wasn't getting married…" Jellia tossed her head. The blood of our Italian ancestors really showed in her dark hair.

"Where did you last see him?"

"Why?"

A lion didn't need an excuse. But a brother did. "So I can check if it's the locket, and if it is, give it back to its owner."

"Just looking for an excuse to see that sorceress again," my sister huffed.

"If her locket is found and returned, then I'll have no excuse to see her anymore. Would that make you happy?"

"Yes." Jellia eyed me. "You're really just tracking jewelry for her?"

I made the devil happy as I lied. "Yup."

Jellia bought the excuse and told me she'd last seen the dude who'd caught the necklace on the shuffle head deck. A small one located at the prow of the ship, well out of the way of passengers and windows.

Just before Jellia left, she paused in the door. "Promise you'll stay away from the witch."

"You want me to stay away from the witch, Dorothy?" I deliberately used the wrong name instead of Jane.

"Yes. Promise me."

"I promise to keep my hands off Dorothy." I earned even more brownie points with Lucifer. Yet what choice did I have? No way was I promising to stay far from Jane.

We had unfinished business. Hence why, the moment my sister left, I hunted down the guy with the locket.

He didn't prove hard to find. Desmond, some kind of lord who claimed he came from an alternate Ha'el dimension, was mourning the loss of his one true love. She'd betrayed him. Been a traitor to his country. Blah. Blah. Blah.

The story had a bevy of women enthralled. Luckily, Jane was not one of them. Jinjur, on the other hand, stared at him raptly.

I sidled close to my sister. "He's not that great." I summed him up, noticing I not only had a few inches on Desmond but that I possessed much better hair.

"It's so tragic. His fiancée was forsaken for her crimes. He can't even speak her name. It's forbidden."

"So he claims." I eyed the handsome fellow with mistrust. Was this the same guy Jellia claimed had caught the locket? He'd dressed in a casual suit, which meant light linen jacket over a thin dress shirt and slacks. It also meant a number of pockets that could hide the necklace.

"I really should introduce cousin Mara to him," Jinjur mused aloud.

"I thought you hated Mara." Theirs was a rivalry that put holes in the walls.

"I do. Which is why she's perfect. He'll date her—not for long because she's the rebound girl—then I'll swoop in to console him. And not feel any guilt that I rescued him from that twat-waffle."

The worst part about her scheme? "That is actually quite a sound plan, but you're forgetting something."

"What?"

"His ex-girlfriend isn't dead. Which means, she's a temptation. I'd be careful if I were you."

"Good point. Maybe we should find out where she lives and make sure she moves on."

I didn't ask Jinjur to elucidate her meaning,

mostly because I didn't want to know if it meant pushing this mystery lady down a set of stairs or simply ensuring that she was fucking someone else.

"You know who might know more about this dude and his ex? Nosy Aunt—"

"Rosy!" Jinjur exclaimed. "I'm going to find her."

With my sister gone, I could now move in on the Romeo.

"Psst," I hissed, trying to distract him from the succubus falling out of her bikini currently offering him a soothing massage.

"What?" Desmond glanced over at me.

"Can I talk to you for a minute?"

"Do we know each other?"

"We do now. Ozmodeus Alexopolous." I held out a hand, and the other man shook it. Firmly. I could feel the strength in him. See the command in his bearing. Good clothes meant possible wealth. All his teeth. I liked him less and less.

"You're a shapeshifter."

"Yup. And you're…" I frowned as I sniffed him. A hint of brimstone and heat. Ashy, smoky heat. But not a demon.

Desmond smirked. "I'm a dark lord. I rule over the demons in Ha'el. And in my world, your kind are nothing but pets." The arrogant smile almost met my fist.

"Did you catch something earlier? Maybe a locket?" I boldly asked. Might as well find out before I tossed his pompous ass overboard.

"You mean this?" It dangled from his fist, and he offered me a cold, tight smile. "It's spelled, you know."

"But do you know what kind of spell?" I paused for effect. "A love spell."

"Despite knowing that, you're here trying to get your paws on it. One wonders why," Desmond mused aloud.

"The witch it's keyed to wants it back."

"And sent you to get it. That's wise. Because what if we were to be smitten with one another? A dark lord and a witch. It could work. Might fix what ails me…" The words trailed off.

Since Desmond wasn't handing the necklace over, I lost patience. I blamed my disbelief and slight panic as the guy appeared to contemplate keeping and using the locket.

That couldn't happen. Wouldn't happen. I refused.

"Hand it over, and no one has to get hurt." Some might call it a threat. I thought of it more as fair warning.

"Do you really think you can take me?" Desmond moved into my space, almost nose-to-nose. But I remained taller. Wider.

I snarled.

He snarled right back.

And then Jinjur was there between us, growling. "Don't you look at my brother like that. Future husband or not, I won't tolerate it."

To his credit, Desmond didn't snap at my sister or lay a hand on her, which made my next move a tad dirty.

"Hey, Jinny, he's got a love locket on him that's gonna choose him a wife." I didn't specify the fact that it was keyed to a particular woman.

Jinny dove for the supposed dark lord. And she wasn't the only one. Women came out of nowhere—a few men, too. The pile-on proved intense and thick. A smart man, I stood on the outskirts, watching as fists flew, hands groped, clothing got ripped…things happened that made me happy this was an adults-only deck.

Once the pile of bodies vanished, Desmond lay dazed, and Jinjur stood over him, scowling.

"I think he's broken."

"Did you find the amulet?" I had a more pressing concern.

"Nope. Thought I felt the chain at one point, but…" She shrugged.

Dropping to my knees, I quickly rummaged through Desmond's pockets as he mumbled, "Erela, why did you forsake me?"

Nothing came from my search. The locket had vanished.

10

JANE: MAYBE I SHOULD JUST SINK THE SHIP.

THE LOCKET HAD ONCE MORE DISAPPEARED. Not for long, I was sure. Its devious magic would keep it in play until it landed on the right man. And given that Oz had been nowhere near it when it soared back onto the boat, I could safely—and a bit sadly—surmise that it wasn't him.

Not that I wanted Oz to be my mate—even if my girly parts still tingled from that unexpected make-out session. The man could kiss, not to mention ooze sex in a manner that drugged all my senses. In a good way. But also, scary.

The fact that I'd lost control staggered me. In that moment, with the kiss and the feel of Oz's body on me being the only thing that mattered, I'd finally understood why I had been conceived in public. Hell, I'd almost recreated history.

Totally out of character. Shocking now that I had a chance to step back and examine what had happened. Surely it wasn't uncontrollable lust making me act irrationally. It had to be the fault of the locket, the spell on it forcing my hormones into overdrive. Convincing my uterus that I needed a man. The magic must be making me horny because no way was this desire for Oz natural.

Even if it weren't real, it gave me the perfect excuse to put morals and history aside to jump in the sack with him. A quick wham-bam-thank-you-ma'am to get Oz out of my system.

Would once be enough?

"Ugh." I groaned aloud, mostly because I couldn't stop thinking about him. "This is pathetic." It didn't help that I'd left him to find privacy in my room. The coffin that only stifled.

I quickly changed out of my damp clothes, opting for a light summer dress and strappy sandals, which by some miracle I'd found in my messy bag after only a little bit of rummaging around.

My damp, frizzy hair irritated in my braids which I'd bunned, so I took the plaits out and ran my fingers through the curls. Go wild, or go home. A cruise, unlike the workplace, was a perfect place to let my hair loose.

I also slid on shorts under my dress. Some of the shorter-stature cruise guests had wandering gazes.

I'd just applied lipstick when I felt something. A flutter in my heart. Not the usual tug of magic, but something that had my pulse racing. The love spell wasn't wasting time. The locket must have found a new victim.

Perhaps I should hunt it down myself and not involve Oz. Each time the locket appeared in his vicinity, it disappeared soon after.

"I'll go without him," I grumbled under my breath, preparing to leave the room.

No, you're not. The voice in my head froze my hand on the door handle.

Swinging it open, I noticed Oz slouching across from my door. At the sight of me, he straightened.

A bunch of things whirled in my head. Questions like, "Why are you stalking me?" "How is it you look so good?" "Want to come inside?" All kinds of brilliant things to say to that handsome hunk of a man. I settled on, "Hey."

"Hey." A single, low syllable in reply.

Look at us, masters of conversation.

He scuffed his big foot and ducked his head. "Thanks for saving me."

Since I wasn't about to admit that I'd panicked when I thought he might die, I replied with, "Don't thank me. Purely mercenary reasons. I need you to help me find that locket." So I could pulverize it and shatter the spell before it put me with someone… who wasn't Oz.

"That locket's pretty important. What's the deal with it?" Oz asked.

"It's cursed." A quick reply as I debated telling him the truth or a version of it.

I walked up the corridor, and he fell into step beside me, the narrowness of the hallway meaning his body brushed mine. Each touch sent a jolt of awareness through me. If he bumped me just a bit harder, I might come before we reached the stairs. I swore my whole body was clenched so tightly, it was a wonder I didn't combust.

"Cursed? Your grandma said something about it leading you to your fiancé?"

"When did you talk to my grandma about me?"

"The first night of the cruise, when she told me to stay away from you."

"I can't believe she's meddling in my business," I huffed. "And after what she already did. Grandma is the one who cursed my necklace."

"How bad can it be? I got the impression she's fond of you."

"She is. Grandma loves me tons, but she's also a meddling biddy, which is why she stole my locket and placed a love spell on it."

"Hardly a curse."

"Says the guy who doesn't have his grandma trying to set him up with a stranger."

He snickered. "Why not use a dating service if you're hard-up?"

My lips pressed into a thin line. "It's not that I can't find a guy on my own. Grandma just thinks I'm being too picky and taking too long."

"Sounds familiar." He pitched his voice when he next said, "You're not getting any younger, Ozzie, so don't be too picky, but be picky enough because you know, the blood." He rolled his eyes.

My lips twitched. "The dark lord forbid I give her a grandbaby with the wrong kind of genes. Bad enough my mother fell for a pirate. Which is why Grandma cast a spell to help me choose the right mate."

"So, the fellow from last night is your mate?"

I shook my head. "The pirate doesn't have the locket anymore."

"Because he tossed it overboard, and that sea monster got it. And came to get you. Meaning, for a moment, he was supposed to be your fiancé. But then the creature returned it to the ship. So, who has it now?"

I eyed him. "You're the mighty tracker. You tell me." Because while my pulse still raced, it told me nothing more. Not a direction or a floor to go looking, which meant I needed Oz's help.

He rolled his impressively broad shoulders. "I haven't had a chance to locate the target since it got returned. My sister wanted to have a chat."

The grimace on his face brought a smirk to mine. "She didn't look too happy."

"She hasn't been happy in months. I swear this wedding business has turned her into a monster. Did you know she expects me to wear shorts for the ceremony? Khaki shorts." Whispered as if it were the worst thing possible.

"Afraid to show off your pasty legs?" Which I already knew to be a lie. I'd seen him naked. His tan went all over. Without lines. As if he spent lots of time outdoors, nude.

"Real men don't wear shorts and loafers and a collared shirt."

"You'll look handsome, I bet." I fed his annoyance, and when he growled, I laughed.

A full-throated chuckle that had him staring at me. Then smiling. "You should do that more often."

"What, insult you?"

"Laugh. Smile. Look happy." We emerged onto a lower deck, and a warm breeze struck my cheek along with a ray of sun.

My light mood was having an effect. "I'm happy." I said it with surprise.

"If you say so. According to your grandmother, you need a mate."

I opened my mouth to lie, which would have totally pleased the dark lord if he listened. But instead, I did something odd. I told the truth. "I don't know if I need a mate, but Grandma's right. I need something more in my life. I'm content, I have a home, my health, my magic. I had a job until Grandma got me fired so she could take me on this trip. But I'm sure I can find another. Technically, I've got everything I need to be happy."

"No boyfriend, though."

"Who says I need a man to be complete?"

"My mother. Although, in my case, she's told me I need a mate to make sure I eat right and get my hair cut so it doesn't go shaggy."

"Who can mow the lawn because the neighbors can't see me using magic on the lawnmower. And carry out the trash." I grinned as I deliberately threw traditionally masculine roles at him.

"You can hire someone for that," he teased. "I, on the other hand, need a mate to ensure I don't forget presents for birthdays and to buy me clothes."

"What's wrong with your clothes?"

"They're comfortable."

Again, my lips quirked. "You mean like your shirt." I poked at the hole over his pectoral.

"The more ragged, the comfier." Said with a grin. He pointed to a set of steep steps. "Let's go to a higher deck where there's a nicer breeze and a view."

I eyed him. "Do I really look like someone who enjoys taking stairs?"

"Are you hinting that I should carry you?"

"Don't you dare carry me."

"I accept the challenge." He swept me into his arms before I could argue. Then I didn't want to. If the lion wanted to show off his strength, let him. It would save my legs and feet.

He began to climb the steps while continuing our conversation. "Why are you without a boyfriend?"

"Why are you single?" I countered.

"Because I haven't met my fated mate."

For some reason, the last bit of that statement bothered. "Fate," I scoffed. "You're talking about the mating instinct."

A chuff of amusement escaped him. I noticed that he wasn't even breathing hard as he made it to the first landing. The stairs were steep. He didn't seem bothered.

"The mating instinct is grossly exaggerated."

"How would you know if you've never experienced it?" I countered.

"Who says I haven't?"

"You're single," I pointed out.

"Could be by choice."

"I've heard when you meet your mate the urge to be with her is irresistible."

He shrugged. "For some, yes, I guess it is. Others

have said it isn't much different from dating other people. And some never get that feeling at all. What of witches? Do you have a certain something that happens when you meet the warlock of your nightmares?"

"No. We make our own choice on who we marry."

"Unless a love spell is involved," Oz reminded, and I grew sullen. He reached the desired deck and set me on my feet. I immediately moved away from him.

Oz remained close. "What will you do if you find the locket? Marry the man who has it in his possession?"

"No."

"Not even if he's the one?"

"I don't want magic to force someone to love me." The admission spilled out of me, and I immediately wanted to take it back. I was a witch. Magic would always be a part of me and my life. What did it matter how I found love?

"It didn't manage to force you with the pirate or the sea monster."

"Because they weren't right for me."

"Then perhaps the next one will be." For some reason, he spat the words out angrily.

"No, it won't. Because I'll make my own choice." I leaned against the rail. "I'm going to remove the spell on the locket and prove to Grandma that I'll be fine on my own. She only cast it in the first place because she worried about me being lonely when she moves out."

"Is she right?" Oz asked, leaning beside me.

"If I say yes, then I sound pathetic."

"What if I told you I'm surrounded by family all the time, yet sometimes I feel alone?" He glanced at me. "Family is all well and good, but as I've gotten older, I find myself looking for something…more."

He stared at me.

I stared at him. The distance between us narrowed, our lips close enough to almost touch.

A frustrated yell emerged from a lower deck. A glance over the railing showed a woman stalking away from a dangling tentacle. The same one we'd tangled with this morning.

It had nothing to do with us, yet the mood evaporated. I put some distance between us, and opened my mouth to give him a lame excuse to leave when Oz said, "Want to be my date to my sister's wedding tonight?"

I blinked. "I thought your sister warned you away from me."

"She warned me away from Dorothy. Not Glinda-slash-Jane."

"You lied to your sister."

"Yes."

"About me? Why?"

He grinned. A dimple appeared. "Because I'd hate to break a promise."

The implication just about knocked me out. "Wouldn't it be easier to do what they want and stay away?"

"Easy, yes. What I want..." He just stared at me. So sexy. His expression intent.

On me. I couldn't lie. It made me zing a little bit. Oz had a way of making me feel special. Of igniting parts of me that shouldn't be paying attention.

Call it weakness or a desire to see what would happen. Whatever it was, I replied with, "Sure."

Which was how I found myself, a few hours later, sitting on the forward deck at sunset, wearing a filmy, powder blue gown that had mysteriously arrived at my door in a boutique bag. No price tag attached, but obviously new. I actually had shoes to go with it, and left my hair down—because Oz had told me he liked it. I did, however, mousse it into a curly fluff. "Go big," my mom had always said. Grandma, too. Yet I'd let myself conform to what was expected of me. Why hide my hair?

Luckily, I avoided Grandma. Explaining my date might have gotten me a lecture. She'd not been too happy when she caught me resuscitating Oz. Then I asked her about Shax.

The conversation had ended mighty quickly after that.

A knock on the door had me catching my breath. Holding it for a second, even.

It was him.

My heart hammered. I was thirty bloody years old, and yet I had the worst case of the butterflies.

It took me forever to open the door, and I wondered if I'd waited too long and if Oz had left.

The door opened to show him leaning on the wall across the hall. He was dressed in those shorts he hated. The collared shirt he'd mentioned. His hair somewhat brushed but with great flow on the sides.

It brought out the naughty. "You look like a very handsome yuppy about to bust out of his clothes."

He tugged at the neckline of his shirt. "I am pretty sure it's choking me."

"Pussy." Softly said. His lips quirked.

"You look beautiful." He practically purred the words, and heat suffused me.

"Thanks." I glanced down at the floor, at his feet, my feet.

He chuckled. "Since when are you shy?"

Since when indeed. My chin snapped up. "This feels weird."

"Did I get the wrong size?"

I shook my head. "Not the dress. It's perfect." As if he knew exactly what would suit me.

"Then what's wrong?"

"It's just… I'm nervous?" It came out almost like a question.

"So am I."

"No way. You're like Mr. Cool and Composed."

He grinned. "Inside, my heart is pounding. I half-thought you wouldn't be here. Or that you wouldn't answer."

"I'm not a coward."

"I know you're not. But you and me—"

I interrupted with a shake of my head. "There's no you and me."

"You keep telling yourself that." His phone went off. An angry *Flight of the Bumblebee* symphony bursting from his pocket.

"Aren't you going to answer?" I asked as he ignored it.

"It's my sister wanting to know where I am and commanding me to move my ass."

"The one getting married?" My eyes widened. "Are you late?"

He had the laziest smile on his lips as if we had all the time in the world. "We're fine. I made sure I came to get you with plenty of time to spare."

"Afraid I'd need convincing?" I teased.

"More because I knew this would happen." He reached for me and drew me close. "I've wanted to repeat our kiss all day."

"That wasn't a kiss," I protested—weakly, I should add.

"Are you sure? Maybe we should try it again." The words hotly brushed my lips, and yet I was the one to close the distance and press my mouth to his.

An instant jolt of…just about everything. I clung to his mouth, my hands flat on his chest, his arms around me, holding me close. The pure maleness of him surrounded me, and I savored it. Ran my hands over the sculpted hardness of his muscles. Felt him shudder at my touch. Heard the soft hums and groans. I affected him. There was no doubting the heady knowledge of realizing that I could make this man want me.

He went to his knees with a moan. "Fuck me, we don't have time for this."

"Pity." I glanced down at him, my panties really wet, my body throbbing. Everything in me wanted to reach for him.

His phone went off again. An even angrier bumblebee.

"We really should go," I murmured.

"I know," he sighed. "But I really don't want to."

I stepped away from him. "Are you sure you still want me to come?"

"Yes. No," Oz growled and raked his fingers through his hair. "I can smell you."

"Thanks." A wry reply.

He made a sound. "No, it's not bad. It's good. Too damned good, and I don't want to share."

Jealousy. It shouldn't have been sexy. I melted a little bit more and just made it worse. Oz's nostrils flared, and he grabbed for me, only I danced out of reach.

"You don't have time for this." I waggled my fingers, sluicing a cool shield of magic around me.

He blinked. "Your scent, it's gone. How?"

"I'm a witch, remember?"

"You can just turn it off?"

"Not exactly off. Just contained so no one else can see or smell."

He stared at me. "You're still aroused?"

I nodded.

He leaned his head back, drew in a deep breath, and shuddered. When he looked at me again, his eyes had a primal gleam to them. "Let's go before Jellia hunts me down and guts us both."

Good thing I'd made that shield thick because putting my hand on his arm felt way more intense than it should have.

We soon ran into people going in the same direction, all of them giving Oz a wide berth. He paid none of them any mind, but he *did* look at me often.

"You kept your hair down."

"I did."

He hummed.

I secretly smiled.

A large ballroom had been given over to perform the ceremony. Space was needed for the hundreds of guests. Way too many bodies crammed into chairs.

"Are those all family?" I hissed.

"Friends, too."

"It's like half the ship."

"A third," he admitted. "There're three more weddings happening after this. None to any more of my sisters, I should add."

We got more than a few glares and stares as Oz escorted me to a spot near the front—which I escaped as soon as he left to move to a place close to the back. As if I'd let him put me out there so prominently. It was one thing to feel stuff for him, another to tell anyone else.

I might have moved, but the seat I chose still gave me an excellent view of him.

Despite his feelings on khaki shorts and collared shirts, he looked good, his broad shoulders stretching the fabric, his legs muscular where they emerged from the cuffs. Yet it was his expression that struck me most.

There was nothing concealed in it. Not at all. Oz stared at me.

For the entire ceremony.

And stupid me, I stared back. How could I not? Something was forming between us. Something electric and tangible. I'd almost call it magic, except that was impossible. A witch didn't have the power to spell a shapeshifter.

But perhaps he had some animal magnetism capable of melting me because as the captain asked the happy couple to repeat the vows, I could hear myself saying them in my head. Even more disturbing, I could have sworn I heard Oz reciting them, too.

And when the captain said, "You may now kiss the bride," I yearned for Oz's mouth. I could have sworn I heard him growl from way at the back.

The newlyweds embraced, and the audience cheered as they ran back down the makeshift aisle with Oz stalking behind them, his intent gaze making me tremble.

He was totally going to kiss me. In front of everyone. And I was okay with it.

Damn it, I wanted it.

If only my arm weren't suddenly yanked.

My grandma hissed. "What are you doing, Janey? It's time to get ready."

For a moment, I was confused. Ready for what? This wasn't my wedding night.

And it never would be with Oz.

"Where are we going?" I asked as Grandma tugged me from the main room into the elevator.

"Where do you think?" she said with a snort, and

I finally realized that she wore a robe. The elevator stopped at the very top floor, and the doors slid open. As she stepped out, Grandma's robe hit the floor, revealing all her naked glory—which had lost its wrinkles and presented perky boobs. She said, "The solstice party is about to start. Get undressed, and quickly. We mustn't be late for the devil."

11

OZ: THE MOON MADE ME DO IT.

Jane left before I could reach her. Exited before I could kiss those perfect lips and find out if she, too, felt the strange connection between us. An impossible link.

A lion shifter and a witch, it shouldn't happen—especially to someone in my position. Yet I couldn't help but want her.

Need her.

The very idea sent a chill through me, especially since our earlier conversation about fated mates. I'd downplayed the concept, partially because I used to believe that it was a huge pile of shit.

An irresistible force that made you want someone so badly, you thought you'd go crazy? A need that almost hurt?

Stupid, right?

So why was I starting to understand it?

And why with Jane? The last person I should feel it for. My family would never stand for it. The pride might very well banish me in shock.

How important was that to me?

Looking out over the gathered crowd, I took stock of the most intimate portion of our family pride. We spanned the country and even parts of the world. Not as many as you'd expect. Low birth rates and those breeding outside our lines diluted our genes. As a strong male, and an important one, a proper match was expected of me, even in these modern times.

But I chafed at the restriction, and I choked in this shirt. I undid a few more buttons. I wasn't alone. The moon outside called us. Teasing our inner beasts.

My lion paced inside. Ready for a wild run. A chase.

The hunt… I already knew I wouldn't be able to resist tracking Jane.

The party got loud as the booze flowed from fountains, literally. My cousin Jeremiah had his face under one of the layers and was drinking to the chants of, "Chug. Chug. Chug."

People began drifting outside, lured by the moon, which rose full and plump in the sky.

My mother, who'd spent most of the reception

regally nodding and smiling, proud of Jellia's match, joined me.

"You're not dancing," she remarked.

"Not drunk enough," I replied. It should be noted that even wasted, my dancing wasn't something anyone should ever attempt.

"Hard to get drunk if you don't have alcohol in your glass." She indicated my water.

My lips quirked. "Oops. Thought it was rum."

"You seem preoccupied. Is everything all right?"

"Just waiting long enough to be polite before I go for my moonlight run."

"Is that all that's perturbing you?" Mother arched a perfectly contoured brow. Blond, like the rest of her. I got my dark hair from my father. He died when I was young.

"What makes you think there's a problem? I'm having a great time." Not a lie. I was when I spent time with Jane. Speaking of which, I wanted to get going before the new owner of the locket ran into her. "Think I'll take a stroll on deck."

I went to move past my mom when she pounced with a low question, "Who is the woman?"

"What woman?" I played dumb.

As usual, it didn't work. "The one you were ogling during the wedding like some randy teenager."

"Just a witch." Who set every one of my senses on fire.

"Just." Mother repeated the word, imbuing it with so much meaning, I almost blurted out all the shit roiling through my mind and heart.

Blathering would only get me hamstrung. "We met on board. I needed a date." I shrugged.

"I hear you've been spending a lot of time with her." That translated to: your sisters tattled on you.

I'd have to tell Mother something. Give an excuse as to why I'd been shirking my family duties. "Jane's got a problem I've been helping with."

"I'll bet you have."

A grown man, a fierce lion, and yet I still blushed at the innuendo. "It's not like that." Not yet. But I had hope. "She lost something, and I'm helping her track it."

"And that's it?"

"What else could it be? She's a witch." And a person. And a woman. I had a hard time trying to shove her into just one hole. She was the sum of many things. Most of which I liked too much.

"You know," my mother said looking at my sister twirling in the arms of her new husband in a dance that had her smiling, "things are changing in the world. Practices once thought taboo are becoming more accepted. The mixing of ideas and bloodlines is producing interesting results. Why, even ancient rivalries are engaging in truce."

"And?"

"And, did you know that a long time ago, witches and shapeshifters used to mate?" She cast me a sly glance.

Since I knew she wanted a reaction out of me, I remained still as stone. "Why did they stop?"

"The usual. Lies. Misunderstandings. Jealousy. It started a feud, which spanned centuries."

"I thought the reason it was forbidden was because we're not compatible." A lie, because I knew that Jane and I would be explosive in bed. It was other things that weren't possible.

"That incompatibility thing arose because witches are magic, and we are the opposite of it. But it can happen with some help."

"I don't know why you're telling me this." Another lie. My mother appeared to be giving me permission.

"You like the witch."

"I do." A soft admission. "However, don't worry, I'm aware of my duty."

"Being with a witch won't prevent you from performing your duty to the pride. Or are you planning to be negligent?"

"Of course, not. But what of continuing our legacy?" It had been drilled into me since I was young that I owed a duty to my ancestors.

My mother freed me from that promise with one statement. "The family name is secure."

"Meaning?" I thought I got the gist of her words, I just didn't quite believe them.

"Follow your heart." With that, she left my side.

Holy shit. I stood statue-still as her permission to explore things with Jane filtered through my dumbfounded brain.

She'd just removed one of the biggest obstacles in my way. Now, there only remained one.

Jane herself.

I had to find her. But first, a tribute to the only goddess a shifter believed in.

The moon hung low in the sky in all her glory. Shining like a beacon, it called to me. It was something no shifter could truly resist. And I was no different. My clothes were shed, and my body began to bulge.

In the beginning, the first time the animal breaks free, the change hurts. The reshaping of bones and flesh, the sudden spurt of fur…it's savage, violent, and painful. Then, as it happens over and over, the agony you once dreaded turns into euphoria. By the time I had finished shifting, I was in the throes of ecstasy and roaring to the sky. My four paws hit the deck, and then I was off. Running with family, friends, feline shapes that I knew well. Then there were other guests.

Wolves sprinted with us, howling and yipping as they raced. Even a dragon joined the fun, swooping across the moon, holding a wing outstretched and trumpeting loudly—Look at me!—doing it over and over, seeking attention despite the fact that he looked nothing like a bat.

There were no trees or parks for us to race through, but the decks provided a track with obstacles that we barreled through and around. Lounge chairs acted as springboards. Railings were vaulted. Any who didn't wish to be trampled knew better than to step outside on a moonlit night.

I started out running with giddy abandon, enjoying the stretch of my legs, the crisp new scents. Perfumes and musk, the smell of a fire burning, and…

Jane.

A whiff of her scent was enough to halt me dead. I lifted my head and inhaled deeply, ignoring the cub that slammed into my backside. He bounced, and the rest of the pride flowed around me. My head angled upward as I traced the origin of the smell. I had to go higher.

A lion excels at climbing, and I soon reached the topmost deck, which proved busy this moonlight-filled night. And not just for shifters.

A bonfire burned brightly at the farthest end, propane-fed but with some added herbs to make it smell good—and give a little buzz. The flames licked high, the glow of them red and orange, illuminating the witches dancing around it.

Naked.

Nudity was a fact of life for shifters and didn't really draw my attention much. Seen one naked body, seen them all—some bits scarring a boy for life.

However, I'd never seen *Jane* naked. Imagined, yes, but in the flesh… I found myself transfixed.

Her crazy, curly hair bounced as she leaped and flowed in the witchy circle. Her limbs were perfect, the skin smooth with youth. The shape of her ideal. Her grace hypnotic.

Jane might be acerbic in words and manner, but her dance proved a thing of agile beauty. It mesmerized me, enough that I padded toward her. But I didn't interrupt.

There was magic in her movements. A spell created by the weaving of the undulating bodies and swirling hair. I sat outside the dancing circle. I knew she saw me. Her gaze sought mine each time she came around, her eyes bright, her skin glistening with a sheen of sweat.

Lucifer rose for a minute in the flames. "That's it, witchies! Dance, dance, dance for the devil. But don't touch. The wife is liable to send a storm to sink you if you try."

Jane paid the devil no mind.

She only had eyes for me.

Because she's mine.

And when the dancers spun away from the flames, moving off into the shadows, Jane came for me, hips swaying, her smile enigmatic. She crouched by me and stroked the fur between my ears.

Yes. Yes. I thought it and rumbled it, my head spooning into her. Nothing like a good scratch to make a big kitty purr.

"I can't believe I'm stroking a pussy instead of a man," she murmured. But her statement held amusement.

I chuffed. It wasn't by choice that I remained a cat. I'd given in too fully to the moon. Her heady magic still ran through me, locking me into this shape for a while longer. I didn't really mind. There was something peaceful and right about having my head in the lap of this woman.

"Times like this, you make it very hard to remember who I am," she murmured. I almost wondered if she knew she'd admitted it aloud.

Did she think I didn't understand? I was fully aware of everything. Understood all too clearly what I'd not seen before.

This was the woman for me. The only one. The

female who consumed my mind. Who'd stolen my heart. Even if my mother hadn't granted permission, I doubted I could have stayed away. Jane tempted me even more than the moon.

She is my mate.

A yawn cracked her jaw, and she wiggled until she lay partially splayed atop me. "It's like sleeping on a warm rug." She buried her face in my fur.

Anyone else, I'd have tossed off and eaten. I'd eat Jane soon, too, but in a way that would have her screaming my name in pleasure. Then I'd take her. Claim her. Make her mine.

But first, we napped, entwined on the deck until the first rays of dawn kissed our skin. Yes, skin. I'd shifted in my sleep and now lay under a splayed Jane.

A nice place to be. Someone had draped a blanket over us, the staff not being new to people camping out on deck.

I stroked my hand down her back, feeling at peace with the world and ignoring the intercom going off with a warning. I had more important things to do, like nuzzle Jane's soft, springy hair.

"Attention all passengers, this is Captain Adexios with a last warning to male guests to please remain indoors or chain yourselves. We're approaching Siren Isle." The island of women who could spell men into being their slaves.

As if their song would affect me. I was the moon's disciple and much too strong-willed to fall for silly mind tricks.

Jane, however, worried. She rose from me, taking the blanket with her. She tucked it around her sarong-style, the loose ends hanging. Being a cat, I batted at them.

"Oz, you need to get inside before the singing starts."

"What I need is for you to come back here." I patted my chest and grinned.

"Oz, this is serious. The cruise was informed last night that one of the sirens is looking for some new men."

"Their magic won't work on me."

"Are you sure?" Such doubt clouded her expression.

As if anything could draw me from my sweet Jane.

I opened my mouth to reply, only the singing started. Soft and haunting, it filled the air, the notes distinct. Such a beautiful song. It called to me.

Me specifically. It told me to come, and I had to answer. I rolled to my feet and began to walk.

"Oz, what are you doing?"

Answering the song, of course. It demanded my presence, and yet my progress was impeded. A glance down showed a scowling countenance.

"Where do you think you're going?" asked the witch.

My witch.

Yet the song compelled me to ignore her. "I must go. My mistress calls." Which sounded wrong. My mistress was in front of me. Yet the music insisted.

"You idiot," she grumbled. "I told you to go inside. We need to restrain you."

"I am not a dog to be leashed." I tried to move around Jane, and she sidestepped to keep blocking my path.

"You're not thinking straight. A siren has bespelled you."

"I cannot be bewitched. I must go." The song demanded I stop dallying. I could hear the splash of others answering the call. I had to join them.

"No. I won't let you do this." Jane threw herself at me, wrapping arms and legs around my body. As if she could stop me. I continued to stride for the rail.

I placed my hand on the railing, ready to vault when soft lips pressed against mine and a voice whispered, "Don't go. Stay with me."

12

JANE: OKAY, SO I KISSED HIM ON PURPOSE THIS TIME.

I DON'T KNOW what possessed me to save Oz from the sirens. Why should I care what happened to him? Let him go to those greedy wenches.

Except, I couldn't let him go. This man was mine. Which made no sense, and yet my mind persisted in the belief that I'd claimed him during that surreal wedding ceremony. A conviction reinforced during the bonfire.

I no longer cared what reasons existed to keep us apart. Screw history and all the taboos. I didn't want to lose Oz, so I pressed my lips against his, willing him to snap out of the spell the siren wove. Offered myself instead.

Then had the agony of waiting to see if I was enough.

He paused, balancing on the rail. One strong

shove of a breeze, a lean too far forward, and we'd plummet.

I whispered again, "Please, Oz. Don't leave me."

A shudder went through him. "Never." His arms came around me, wrapping me tight. His lips parted, and I felt the erotic thrust of his tongue. It was electrifying. Arousing. The most intense thing I'd ever experienced. And I wanted more. I'd wasted enough time denying what I needed. No more.

The kiss deepened as we teetered on the rail, and I gasped when we swayed too far. Oz didn't let us fall. He managed to keep us upright, his hands cupping my ass. He started kissing my ear.

A weak spot. I groaned and squirmed.

He groaned right back. "This isn't exactly the spot to be doing that."

No kidding. "We need a bed," I whispered into Oz's mouth. And not the puny one in my cabin. I doubted he'd fit.

"Okay," was his murmured reply before he stepped off the rail.

I screamed into his mouth as we plummeted, not very far as it turned out. He held me tightly as he landed on a balcony below us and kept holding me as he entered someone's room through the sliding glass door.

"What if there's someone here already?" Not the scariest of thoughts. My only concern right now was how long it would be before I could get Oz inside me, doing something about the raging heat consuming my body.

"Better not be anyone here since it's my room."

A peek around showed a lavish suite. Huge and expensive. "Um, are you rich or something?"

"Or something," he said, not quite answering, and then I didn't care because he tossed me onto a very large bed, whereupon I bounced and almost fell off.

He caught me. Pinned me with that deliciously heavy body of his. His lips devoured mine.

Sucking and teasing. His tongue slid into my mouth for an erotic dance that had me moaning and squirming. Even better, no clothes were in the way.

I could feel him against me, his skin scorching hot. Hotter than a mundane man. Digging my fingers into his biceps meant noticing the bulk of his muscles. So many dips and ridges.

The thought of them sent moisture and a jolt of pleasure between my legs.

"Fuck me, Jane, you are way too sexy." The words were growled against my lips.

Me, too sexy? Cute, pretty hot, but the way he said *sexy*… That caused a mini-orgasm, and I clutched him tighter. My mouth plastered to his, our tongues danced in a wet duel that ended abruptly. But only so he could plant hot kisses on my neck. Nips and licks of skin that sent shivers down my spine as he located my sensitive spots and sucked them.

While he teased me, his hands roamed my body, tickling my skin with the rough pads of his fingers, rasping along my taut nipples before he cupped my breasts. He squeezed, and his thumbs dragged back and forth over the buds, drawing a groan from me.

And I did a lot more groaning as he bent his head to take a tip into his mouth, latching on and sucking, the tugs of his hot lips sending quivers through me. I panted and couldn't help but cry out as I clung to his broad shoulders. My fingers dug into the hard muscle, deeper and deeper as pleasure coiled.

And then he moved from my breasts. I would have complained, except he slid down my body until he knelt between my legs. I couldn't help but shudder. I knew what he planned to do next. Was it any wonder my body quivered?

He lifted my leg high enough that he could place a kiss on the inside of my knee. A kiss he dragged up the length of my thigh, the rough bristle of his jaw rubbing along my soft skin.

I clutched at the sheets on his bed, panting and trying not to writhe out of control.

"Touch me. Kiss me. Do something," I groaned as he lowered the left leg to do the same thing to the right.

"Do what?" His warm breath brushed against the moist lips of my sex.

"Taste me."

"If I start licking your cream, I won't stop until you come."

"And that's supposed to be a problem?" I writhed now because my need had reached the point of no return. "Touch me."

"What if I want to savor the sight and smell of your arousal?"

A peek down at him showed him seriously staring at me, his eyes smoldering with passion.

"Lick me." I'd reached the point of begging.

"With pleasure," he growled before diving onto my flesh. The sudden anticipated latch drew a sharp cry from me, and I arched.

A big and heavy hand pinned me back down, leaving me at the mercy of Oz's tongue. He swiped at my sex, lapped at my honey, spread my lips and groaned against my flesh with true enjoyment.

He wasn't the only one enjoying it.

I was beyond coherent speech. Awash in pleasure. My body coiled tight as a spring ready to pop.

His tongue flicked at my clit, and I yelled, then gasped as he slid two fingers into me. Long, hard digits, something for me to clench as he continued to caress my swollen button. Flick. Suck. Nudge. And then he thrust, in and out, increasing the intensity, making me clench until my orgasm tore through me. Still, he kept licking and thrusting with those fingers, drawing out my climax, rolling me into the start of another.

"Fuck me," I sobbed. I wanted him inside, filling me, claiming me.

"With pleasure," he murmured in a husky voice, and I was more than ready. He moved on top of me, the tip of him probing, and I dug my fingers into his flesh, urging him.

Only something chose that moment to rock the ship.

We paused, my flesh throbbing, his cock pressing. The timing *really* bad.

"Think it's the sea monster?" I asked as the ship bobbed again.

"Better not be. Fucking cock-blocker if it is."

Oz's frustration brought a smile.

The intercom speaker inside the room blared to life. "Sorry to interrupt, passengers. Please brace yourselves. We've entered DJ's Locker, and there seems to be some unexpected turbulence."

"Uh-oh." I shoved at Oz, who rolled off me with a puzzled frown.

"What's wrong?"

"I need to go. Now." I hopped from his bed and snared a loose shirt—having left all my clothes on the top deck when I stripped the night before.

"Where are you going?" Oz growled. His eyes glowed gold, and his cock jutted forth, still aching for its turn.

A turn he wouldn't get as the ship rocked again.

"Trust me when I say it's best if I go." Because the thing rocking the ship and cursing with every crashing wave?

Daddy.

We'd arrive at the site of his grave, the seat of his power, and judging by the rough seas? He wasn't happy that someone was fooling around with his little girl.

13

OZ: WHY AM I SUDDENLY HEARING THE THEME SONG TO JAWS?

JANE TOOK OFF, practically sprinting out my suite door, wearing my shirt and nothing else. But that wasn't the reason I roared—the first time because I really liked that shirt. The second louder because she'd left me blue-balled and frustrated. Even now, lying on my back, my cock jutted.

Whined.

Ached.

Yet it wasn't in me to beg. Although the temptation was strong with the flavor of Jane still on my tongue.

She'd tasted so fucking sweet. Sweeter than I expected. I craved more. Of her. Her honey. Her skin. I could still feel the tremors as she came for me on my fingers and against my mouth.

I wanted more. The need hurt almost as much as my pride. Because she'd run out of here as if she'd seen a monster. Surely not...

I glanced down at my erection. Did she fear it? Big, but not *that* big. It had to be something else.

"Fuck."

"You'd better not be planning to fuck my Jane."

The sudden voice, deep and gravelly, didn't belong in my room. It sent me diving from the bed, landing in a crouch, my lip pulled back in a snarl. A figure, leaving a puddle of water on the floor, presented itself at my balcony door but didn't cross the threshold. He wore an old-style waistcoat with large, brass buttons, a hat that drooped, the plume on it a soggy mess. His dark beard dripped, and his eyes flashed, a thunderstorm brewing in the glare.

"Who are you?" I snapped. Jane had claimed that she didn't have a boyfriend. Yet who else would dare call her "my Jane?" Was this the next holder of the locket?

"I am Theodore Davey, the very angry father of the woman you just tried to defile." The man held himself straight, and despite his soaked demeanor, he oozed menace.

"Father?" I just about groaned with my shitty luck.

"Did you think me dead just because my ship

sank and I drowned with all my crew?" The man began to pace on the balcony outside, and with each step of squelching boots, the boat rocked. "I didn't have a choice. The curse finally caught me, and now I must take my turn ruling Davey Jones' Locker."

"The graveyard of sunken ships?" I didn't know much ocean lore, but I'd seen *Pirates of the Caribbean*.

The pirate flourished a hand dripping lace and seawater. "I am the master of these seas. And father of the witch you seduced."

Would it help my cause or ruin it to admit that Jane had initiated the kiss? "I didn't mean any disrespect. I like your daughter…sir." I thought it best to tack that on.

"Do you really think that excuses your behavior?" The man snorted. "You put your depraved paws on my daughter. Don't deny it. The ocean sees all." Theodore ogled me.

I could only shrug. "If it sees all, then you know she kissed me first." I put it out there, and as expected, it didn't work in my favor.

Lightning crackled in the pirate's gaze, and the ship rocked ominously. "Infidel! I'll gut you and feed you to the fish."

I believed him. He seemed very capable of slicing me to pieces with the saber hanging by his side. How confident did you have to be to show up in a lion shifter's room, hands empty? I should tread carefully, especially since Jane probably wouldn't appreciate me hurting her dad, even if her father tried to carve me up first. "We should discuss this like gentlemen."

Theodore recoiled. "You would insult me and call me weak?"

"I didn't mean that as an insult." Since when was gentlemen a bad word? I tried to recover as the pirate advanced on me, his tall leather boots squelching on the floor.

"I will start with your arm so that I might beat you with it." The threat only missed a piratey, "*Arrrr!*" at the end.

I scrambled for a way to get out of this that didn't involve bodily harm to either of us. "Jane will be mad if you hurt me." At least I hoped she would be.

"She'll get over it. It's for her own good," the drowned pirate huffed.

"Keeping her single?" I dared to query.

Theodore paused. "You're not meant to be with her."

"What makes you so sure of that?"

The expression on Theodore's face turned sly. "Because you don't have the locket."

"Maybe she doesn't need the locket to find the right man."

"You can't fight the magic, *boy*." Said with a smug sneer. "The necklace will lead Jane to her true mate."

It better not, because then I'd have to gut the fellow.

Huh? What?

Distracted by myself, I missed Theodore Davey's next words.

"…do you understand?"

I blinked. "I'm assuming you made some kind of threat regarding staying away from your daughter. And I'm afraid I can't promise that." Something existed between Jane and me. A possibility that deserved further exploration.

The cruise ship rocked hard, teetering enough that my bare toes sank into the carpet to hold me from sliding. Hard to look tough when you were trying not to stumble.

Jane's dad grinned, an expression wide and full of teeth—too many of them, and some pointed. I heard the theme song from a certain shark movie playing loudly in my head. The wet, dripping beard and sagging hat did not detract from the evilness of his countenance at all. "You don't want to mess with me while on the ocean, boy. I've sunk bigger ships than this."

"Seems kind of drastic. Why not let Jane decide what she wants?" Could be she'd choose me.

She better. Rawr.

The reaction of my inner feline distracted.

Her daddy snorted. "We tried letting Jane figure things out. But she's challenging. Which is why I agreed to her grandmother's foolish plan with the locket. A locket not in your possession."

"So what? Apparently, I don't need it because I've already got Jane. And I don't find her challenging at all." Which sounded bad out loud, but mostly meant that whatever traits her father worried about were a part of her. People weren't perfect. Their very foibles made them unique. Like me and my need to lick the bowl when I had ice cream. Forgetting and leaving the toilet seat upright. Oh, and I liked to mow the lawn naked.

"You obviously haven't spent time with her," Theodore muttered.

"If you're implying I haven't seen her in a mood, then let me reassure you. She didn't like me one bit when she met me."

"Yet you tricked her into changing her mind."

"No trick. We like each other."

The pirate stared at me. "You seriously can't be that dense. It doesn't matter if you think you do. Save yourself the effort. You don't have the locket, which means you're not the guy she's going to end up with."

"You can't be sure of that."

"Can't I?" The pirate arched a brow. "My mother-in-law might be many things, but she's an accomplished witch, and if she claims she cast a spell that will bring my daughter together with the right person, then it will. And nothing you do or say, will change that."

"Says you. What if the magic is wrong?"

"Wrong?" Theodore Davey chuckled, and the ocean laughed with him, jiggling the boat. "Pity you aren't the one. You're kind of entertaining."

My mane did a bit of a flip as my inner kitty got agitated, tired of not being taken seriously. I really needed Theodore to stop claiming that Jane belonged to someone else. "I don't care about the damn locket. I don't need the fucking thing. I'm going to mate with Jane. *Sir.*" I'd said it out loud. Holy fuck. The shock didn't negate the realization that it sounded so right.

The claim widened Theodore's eyes. "What did you just say?"

"She's mine." I'd never been surer of anything.

"Jane is a witch."

"I don't care."

"Her mother will care. Pairings between shifters and witches are most often childless."

"Then we'll adopt." I kept throwing out answers, excuses to do the things I'd been dancing around since the moment I met Jane. "She's my mate." It got easier and easier to admit.

"Not for long." The pirate's scowl brought the seas to a standstill. In the hush that fell, he said in a deep voice, "As the commander of DJ's Locker, and master of these seas, for the crime of defiling my daughter, I declare you guilty. Prepare to walk the plank!"

14

JANE: DADDY, LEAVE MY BOYFRIEND ALONE.

The moment I left Oz—naked and horny, wearing only his shirt—I ran to the closest public railing I could find and shouted at the raging ocean. "Daddy, you stop this. Right now."

The seas continued to toss.

I shook my fist. "I'm not a little girl anymore! I am a grown woman, and I can do what I like with who I like."

Rather than my father answering, my mother appeared, rising from the waves. The water sluiced from her curvy frame, leaving her dry and yet still inappropriate in an outfit more suited to a tavern wench than my mom.

I averted my gaze and said, "Couldn't you at least wear a bra, Mom? I don't want to see your nipples."

"How did I raise such a prude?" my mother chided. "The body is a beautiful thing."

"Other people's bodies are. Seeing you half-naked is just wrong." And I'd already seen more than enough to last me a lifetime.

"You're one to talk. Miss I'm wearing a man's shirt and nothing else."

Heat filled my cheeks. "I was in a rush."

"You'd better change before your father sees you." A wave rose over the ship's railing and soaked me. I sputtered and choked, yet once the water receded, I found myself dressed in a modest version of my mom's outfit. Buttoned to the neck. Don't ask how. I didn't understand it either.

I still had my back turned on my mother. "Are you decent yet?" I asked.

"Oh, for Neptune's sake." I heard a huff of annoyance, then a whoosh of water. "Is this better?"

When I dared to peek at my mom, she'd added a vest on top of the blouse. "Much."

"Good. Now, come here and hug me."

I knew my mother was dead, and the body in front of me was no longer the same one that had birthed me. I didn't care. I ran into her arms for a hug I'd not realized I missed until now. How long since my last visit? Too long.

I burst into tears.

My mother patted my back. "Really, Jane. Tears?"

"I miss you," I sniffled.

"We talk every week."

"It's not the same." My lower lip jutted in a proper sulk.

"You know the curse that finally caught up to your father makes it impossible for us to leave the ocean, but you're always welcome to visit."

"Don't you miss me?" I asked.

"Of course, I do, darling." She rubbed my cheek. "But in life, as in unlife, things change. People have to move on."

"So everyone keeps saying," I grumbled. "First you and Dad, now Grandma. Why do people keep leaving me? Have I done something wrong?" Something to push them away?

"Oh, Janey. It's not because of anything you've done, it's more because you're all grown up. You don't need us in your everyday life anymore."

"Says you."

"Says your mother." She stroked my hair. "You are doing perfectly fine on your own."

"Then why do I feel like something's missing?" Said in a soft voice. Even as I asked, I saw Oz in my mind's eye.

"My poor, Janey." Her expression softened. "This is why your father and I helped my mother with the spell she cast. Because while you are a beautiful, strong, independent woman, you don't enjoy being alone. You really are happiest with someone around you."

"That's a lie. I'm not a people person."

"This has nothing to do with being social. You are looking for a mate."

"I don't need a man to complete me."

"Are you sure? I know I feel more whole with Theo than I did when I was alone. He is the thing that makes me happy."

"Don't I make you happy?"

She stroked my hair again. "Of course, my sweet Jane. But the love of a mate is different than a child. With children, you always know they will eventually leave to forge their own path. But a husband or wife, a best friend, a lover…they are forever."

Forever. It sounded like a long time. "Spelling the locket means you don't trust me to choose this supposed perfect mate for myself."

"Is that what you think the spell does? Chooses for you?" My mother laughed, the sound similar to tinkling raindrops . "You obviously don't understand how the charm works. Love can't be compelled."

"Then what are you expecting to accomplish with the locket?"

My mother's tone was matter-of-fact. "Lead you to someone you could love, of course. But it will always be your choice."

"So far, that locket led me to a drunken pirate and a sea monster."

Mother tittered. "Your father doesn't know if he should be glad or insulted that you didn't fall for the first."

"He looked a lot like dad, but his beard wasn't fluffy."

"Neither was Theo's," Mother said with a sigh. "I still remember the first time I saw your father. It was at an engagement party."

"Whose?" I asked, not recalling having heard this story before.

"Mine." Her lips curved. "Before I became a pirate's wench, I was engaged to marry some fancy duke."

"How?"

"Because my mother and father weren't gentry." She smiled. "I was a witch. It wasn't hard to set myself up in a proper position and then find myself engaged to a nice-enough man. Handsome and rich."

"Before you could get married, Daddy kidnapped you."

"Actually, he kidnapped me right after the marriage but before the consummation."

"Wait, you were *married*?"

"In name only." Mom's lips curved. "I made sure your father rescued me. From the moment I saw him at my engagement ball, oozing with danger, I knew I wanted him."

"Then why get married to the duke at all?"

Mother rolled a shoulder coquettishly. "Can you think of anything more dashing than a rescue? I'd rendezvoused with your father a few times after that ball. Enough to know that he was the one for me. But I wouldn't call off my engagement. Your father couldn't stand the fact that another man was marrying me. He stole me during the reception and sailed us away on his ship."

"And you fell in love."

"We did."

"And when did you and Dad get married."

She chewed her lower lip.

"Mom?" I prodded.

"It didn't seem important given how we felt about each other."

I gaped at her. "I'm illegitimate."

"Doesn't really matter in this day and age." She smiled hopefully.

I sighed. "I'm a freaking bastard. Just lovely."

"Not the moral of my story."

"What is? Because I am pretty sure it got lost in the rambling."

"I was basically talking about how sometimes you know what you want, even if there are those who say you shouldn't. You like that boy."

"What boy?" I played dumb.

Mother smiled. "You like him. And that's okay."

"He's not a warlock."

"Do you care?"

"Not really." The very thought of Oz filled my mind. Was he still in bed, waiting for me to return?

"Who cares if you're not supposed to be together. Many would say I shouldn't have hooked up with a pirate. I would have missed out on so much if I'd listened. So, do what feels right. What makes you happy."

"And how am I supposed to figure out what that is?" What if it wasn't Oz? Making the wrong choice seemed as scary as continuing the way I was.

"If you're not sure, then find the locket," was Mom's advice as she stepped towards the rail and the rising wave that came to greet her.

My mother was leaving already, her skin drying out from being on deck too long. The curse didn't let either of my parents leave the sea for extended periods.

I ran for her. One last hug. She whispered, "Follow your heart."

My heart wanted a lion. But did Oz really want me? More and more I feared it was the locket making him think he desired me. What if the magic affected him and he didn't realize it? What if he didn't like me as much as I liked him? I wasn't an easy person to love.

"You are perfect." It was as if Mother had read my mind.

We parted, and she smiled at me as the wave began to lower. I noticed that the sea had stopped churning. A strange calm filled the air. I also realized something else. I'd not seen my father yet. Surely, he wouldn't miss a chance to hug his little girl? "Where's Daddy?"

The wave paused, and my mother appeared nervous. "He's around."

"Where?" A knot formed in my stomach. Then the truth hit me. Mother knew about Oz. If she knew… I gaped at her. "Oh, please tell me he doesn't know."

"What did you expect?" Mother held out her hands. "I tried to stop him, but when he heard you crying out…"

I blushed fifty thousand shades of red. "I was yelling because I was um…er…"

"Having an orgasm. I know. And so does your father, which was why he snapped."

That didn't bode well. "What did Daddy do?"

"He didn't sink the ship."

A positive sign. "So he's sulking in the Locker?"

"Not exactly," Mother hedged. "He paid the ship a visit."

"He didn't visit me." Only, as I said it, my eyes widened. "Where is Daddy?"

"Where do you think?"

My eyes rounded more. "No. Oh, no. Please say he didn't go after Oz."

"Really, honey, what did you expect? And with a shifter of all things." My mother tsked. The woman who fell in love with a pirate chiding me?

"It was just oral." Good oral, and it would have been epic sex.

"A shame then that he's not the one."

"How do you know?" I asked. A shocking question, because when I was with him, it felt just right.

"Because if he were your true mate, you wouldn't still be talking to me. You'd be saving him from your father."

The realization that I wasted time galvanized me into motion. Daddy confronting Oz could only mean one thing.

"Daddy!" I yelled his name. "Don't you dare make Oz walk the plank."

15

OZ: SWAN DIVE OR CANNONBALL?

As I stood on the edge of an actual plank suspended over an ocean that currently teemed with jagged fins, it occurred to me that I should probably be taking the situation more seriously. But instead, curiosity once more was my companion, and it wondered...where did the pirate find a plank in the middle of the sea? And did he keep those lion-eating sharks as pets? Because I had a saltwater pool at home that no one in the pride used—the whole hate of water-slash-swimming thing—and it would make a great home for a denizen of the deep. It even had a diving board that we could make our enemies walk.

Because how cool was it to be told to walk the plank? It was like the fantasy from every pirate movie ever. I truly hoped someone live-streamed this so I could watch it later.

If I survived. Because Theodore Davey—pirate and pissed-off father of one Jane Davey—didn't seem interested in forgiveness as he presided over the gathering crowd.

"So, let me get this straight. Anyone who tries to make out with your daughter will get thrown to the sharks?" someone in the mob of faces yelled.

"Yes," Captain Davey said flatly.

"What if he just holds her hand?" hollered someone else.

"Then he loses it."

There was a murmur, and then a *thunk* as something came sailing from the crowd and landed on the deck by Davey's feet. A golden object that glinted when the pirate lifted it with the tip of his sabre.

A locket dangled from the chain. Wouldn't you know the damned thing would resurface now to taunt me.

"Ah, shit. My wife is going to kill me," Davey grumbled. "Surely someone in the audience wants to date my darling girl."

The crowd leaned away, and no one said a word.

"I would," I offered.

"Not talking to you, fleabag. Anyone?" Davey shook the amulet.

All he got in reply was the shrill shriek of my sister. "Ozzie, get down from there. The safety manual specifically said no swimming with the sharks." Jellia shoved her way through the bodies until she stood at the front of the crowd, Jinjur close behind.

"Your brother is going to walk that plank." Davey turned to me. "Aren't you?"

I shrugged. "If it makes you feel like a bigger man." Taunting a pirate. What could I say? I lived on the edge. A glance down showed that to be quite literal.

"I'm going to enjoy watching you get eaten." Davey pointed his sword. "Jump."

"Don't you dare obey that order." Jinjur took a step towards Davey and flexed her claws. "Ozzie, get down."

"Ozzie," the pirate said in a mocking tone, "isn't going anywhere. He's my prisoner."

My sister planted her hands on her hips and huffed. "Oh no, he's not. He's supposed to be the uncle who spoils my future cubs rotten. Unhand my brother."

"He must pay for his crimes."

"What crimes?" asked Jinjur. "Bad hair? Happens to even the lushest of manes in the ocean air."

A reminder that I'd not bothered to run a brush through it. But at least I'd grabbed some pants, or I'd be standing in the buff, making everyone feel inadequate.

Davey sneered. "Your brother is a defiler. Guilty

JANE DAVEY'S LOCKET

of leading my daughter into sin."

"A pirate pontificating about sin. Ha!" Regal as a queen, my mother strode through the crowd, which parted for her before she even got close. Rumors must have gotten around about her sharp claws.

"Madam, I don't believe we've had the pleasure." Theodore swept off his plumed hat and presented a deep bow.

"Don't you waggle that beard and make flirty eyes with me. I know you're married."

"Alas, my heart is taken by a most demanding wench, but my first mate's isn't," Davey offered.

"Not interested in negotiating, given that's my son you've got standing on that plank."

"On the contrary, it would seem I have something you want." Theodore practically purred the words. Impressive for a dead guy.

"I want you to go back to the ocean and leave my son alone. Or else." Mother growled, and her eyes glowed. Never threaten a lioness's cub. Never mind the fact that I was a grown-ass man on the other side of thirty.

I looked down at the churning water. Getting torn to pieces might be preferable to this humiliation.

"I don't need your help, Mom," I grumbled. "I was handling this."

"You call standing on the edge of death *handling*

it?" Mother shrieked.

"Captain Davey has a valid reason. He caught me messing around with Jane."

"And?"

Davey cleared his throat. "And it is a crime to defile my daughter." Some of my manhood returned at the accusation.

"Defiled, ha. Try flipping that around, Captain Soggy Bear. I've seen your daughter. Throwing herself at him. No better than a hussy." My mother sniffed.

Before Davey could take offense, I did. "Take that back. I won't have you speaking about Jane like that."

"What? You'd take the side of the witch over me?" Mother grabbed her chest.

"Her name is Jane, Mom."

"Her name doesn't matter, nor this farce of justice."

"I am king of these waters!" boomed Davey.

"And I am his mother." The finger jabbed in my direction. Once more, my manhood shrank.

"Then feel free to join him on that plank." Davey swept a hand, the locket still dangling from it.

A pendant I needed to get my paws on.

"Daddy! Where are you, Daddy?" The strident cry was heard before I caught sight of the wielder of the voice. But it wasn't long before I caught a glimpse.

My witch stalked the deck, flinging her hands left

and right, tossing people out of her way. When the shifters she tried to move remained standing, her magic breaking apart on their frames, she waggled her digits and grabbed someone who was affected and slammed them into the unmoving person.

Effective and smart. Also, very hot.

"Hey, Glinda." I waved. "What happened to my shirt?" Not that I minded her current look. She wore a long, loose skirt and a blouse tucked in, every inch of her covered like a present that needed unwrapping. I liked gifts.

"Sorry about my dad. You can get off that plank," Jane said in a rush of words.

Davey cleared his throat. "Don't you dare move, boy."

"You did not just seriously say that." Jane came to a halt in front of her father, brows arched and arms crossed. "Exactly, what do you think you're doing?"

"Don't you dare blame this situation on me. I came to say hello to my precious little girl, only to realize unspeakable things were being done to her."

Jane's lips quirked. "I couldn't speak because I was enjoying it."

My manhood completely revived and gained some ground at her claim.

"No. No. No." Davey shook his head. "You did not just say that. My precious daughter is an untouched maiden."

"I haven't been a virgin in a long time, Daddy." Jane appeared to take great satisfaction in the announcement.

"Jane Theodora Davey." Her father shook his finger. "You and I will be having a chat about virtue. Right after this fellow walks to his doom." The scowl turned my way and contained a little shove, a gust of wind suddenly slamming into me. Apparently, undead magic worked just fine on a lion shifter.

I found myself teetering on the edge of the plank, counting fins. The damned sharks wouldn't stop moving though, meaning my ballpark of fifty might be a little high. Or low. I couldn't really tell.

"Oz!" Jane yelled my name.

"Don't worry. I got this." How bad could wrestling sharks be? And I'd have help.

I heard Jellia say in the background, "Someone hold my sunglasses." The equivalent of a beer.

"You are not walking the plank, Oz. Do you hear me, Daddy? Oz is..." Jane's voice trailed off. "What is that in your hand? Is that my locket? Hand it over."

I peered over my shoulder to see her hand outstretched, beckoning.

Davey tucked it behind his back. "You know I can't do that. Your mother would kill me."

"Don't involve me in this. This fiasco was your idea." A wave rose on Theodore's left and deposited a woman on deck. Given her resemblance to Jane, it didn't take much to guess that I was meeting Mrs. Davey.

"We both know he's not the man for her. This,"—Davey shook the locket—"will lead her to the right man."

"I don't want it to." Jane stamped her foot. "Give it so I can break the spell."

"No." Davey tucked his other hand behind his back and held the locket tight. "I'll find another pirate to give it to. A less drunk one this time."

Jane screeched. "Don't you dare!"

"Enough of this." Jane's mother swept close to the pirate and held out her hand. "Give it."

"I swear, I know a better pirate. Handsome. Still alive. Has his own boat."

Mrs. Davey's fingers waggled.

The dreaded pirate sighed as he held out the chain, the locket on it spinning, in front of more than a few cats.

Jinjur, Jellia, my mother, and a few others who crowded close to the spectacle tracked it. Back and forth. Dangle. Twist.

Swat. No surprise, a few paws batted at the shiny thing, knocking it from the pirate's grip.

It fell, right into the midst of the churning fins.

Only one thing to do.

I jumped in after it.

16

JANE: THE THINGS I DO FOR LOVE.

For a moment, after the idiot had jumped, there was stunned silence. Then a flurry of clothes flying and bodies leaping for the rail. There went Oz's sisters, his mother, and who I assumed were other family members after him, turning the waters into a chaotic mess.

I glared at my dad. "Are you happy now?"

"That depends. Are you mad?" My dad sidled closer to the edge, his nervous sweat keeping him damp.

"You made my boyfriend walk the plank."

"It should be noted that he jumped of his own volition."

Doubtful. I was more convinced than ever that the locket was having an effect on Oz.

"Take note of the fact, D*addy*," I said his name with a snarl, "that I'm going after him."

Despite knowing that I might die and get stuck with my parents, I jumped. Straight-bodied, I plummeted down, closing my eyes to the churn below me. The hooting. The hollering. The splashing. The… shark that hit me midair and tumbled me upside down.

I hit the water with my mouth open and swallowed some. The problem with coughing? I couldn't catch a breath. Too much ocean.

My lungs tightened. Fear rose in me. Annoyance, too.

Drowning really wasn't what I had planned, and I was feeling pretty testy at the moment. Not to mention, I was in my element. The seat of my daddy's power. It meant this princess of DJ's Locker wasn't without some skills.

I swirled my finger in the water and pushed some magic into the motion. Pushed and pushed, widening the swirl, the water spiraling with it, turning into a reverse cyclone made of water and fury.

Kind of satisfying on a primal, visceral level.

As the water spun, it caught the cruise line passengers and sharks alike, sending them spinning. Every now and then, a head popped out for an excited scream of, "Yeehaw!" or a less than pleased, "I'm gonna puke!" Then some shrieks when someone did.

The maelstrom kept churning until it reached the bottom of the ocean and cleared the water from the ship sunken there.

The *Sweet Jeanine*. Named after my mom. My parents' home. I stood on the weathered deck, ignoring the flopping fish and gasping coral. Noticed some engravings done in metal and kept tarnish free on the wall leading to the cabin. Images of me. And Mom. My family.

Aw, how cute.

But distracting. I glanced back at the whirlpool and noticed that I had some help.

People began to pop free of the wall of water, and an arm of liquid carried them back to the *Sushi Lover*. All of the passengers were rescued, courtesy of my mother, while I concentrated on Oz.

Unlike the others, he still played with the sharks, coasting to the ones caught in the spin, wrestling them, and then wrenching their mouths open before shoving his fist inside. Not finding what he wanted, he'd then heave the shark from the whirlpool and head for another.

I knew what he looked for.

And when he found it, he kicked free of the spinning vortex and landed with knees bent on the deck of my parents' ship. He stood, and the damned locket dangled from his fist.

He smiled wider than the kitty in Wonderland. Smugger than the one who got into the cream.

"Oh, Jane," he crooned. "Look what I found."

I saw it, the necklace dangling from his grip, the spell obviously working its magic on him despite his shifter heritage. But I ignored it in that moment to admire the crazy bastard who'd jumped off a ship into a pile of sharks to wrestle them to find it.

There was no surprise that Oz swept me into a distracting kiss. Potent enough that I began to lose my grip on the magic and water rushed in. It smothered us, and I retained enough sense to propel us to the surface where we burst free of the water, hugging each other, our lips meshed, our temperatures rising. We landed on the deck of the cruise ship where there was hushed silence and then a roar as people cheered.

Not everyone was happy. When I finally broke the kiss, it was to see my father glowering. "I can't believe you went after him."

"What did you expect?"

"That you'd remember who you are."

A woman in love? I was well aware. And, apparently, I wasn't the only one annoyed that everyone kept telling us to stay apart.

Oz growled. "I swear, the next person who says we can't be together is getting his face chewed off."

"You tell them, Ozzie," Jinjur hollered. "You're a king. No one can boss you around."

A king? I eyed Oz. "What's she talking about? Is this like the whole lions are king of the jungle thing or…?"

Jinjur giggled. "More like he's king of the South Coast pride."

"He presides over the bottom ten states including Texas," his mother announced with pleasure.

I felt faint. "You can't be a king."

"King and a, like, billionaire. He paid for the entire wedding," Jellia announced.

"You're rich, too?" I shopped the bargains whenever I went out.

"It's not a big deal," Oz muttered.

Yet, it was. He was a person of import. A big deal. Oh, damn. Wouldn't you know, all of a sudden, my daddy was singing a different tune.

"Southern states, eh? They've got some nice beaches."

"Indeed, they do. I own a house in east Texas along the shore. With a pier that goes out to some fairly deep water."

As my father suddenly found interest in Oz, I retreated, only to be stopped by Jellia. "I can't believe he called it a house. More like a castle." His sister snickered.

"I can't live in a castle." I was used to living in cozy spaces. To a cramped kitchen where I bumped hips with Grandma when she cooked. A small couch perfect for sharing a cozy blanket while mocking episodes of *Sabrina the Teenage Witch*. A castle… would we even share the same bedroom, or be on opposite ends of the dwelling? Panic filled me.

As if sensing my unease, Oz turned his attention on me. "You can choose from any of the properties."

"You own more than one home?"

"If you don't like any of them, then we'll buy a few more."

The casualness had me almost hyperventilating as I panicked.

Good thing Mother was there to whisper, "They're just things. It's who you're with that counts most."

She had a point. Did I care about rank and wealth if I got to be with Oz?

He chose that moment to smile at me, teeth gleaming. His hair was slick and sexy, framing his face.

The locket hung around his neck.

Which was probably why he said to my dad, "Sir, I'll probably never get a better chance to ask permission for your daughter's hand."

It took my dad being elbowed by my mother before he said, "I guess you can marry her."

The spell had worked. I was engaged.

I fainted.

17

OZ: WHO'S GOT THE PRETTY SHINY? I GOT THE PRETTY SHINY.

Jane never hit the deck because I caught her.

But her father panicked. "What's wrong with her? Janey! Speak to your daddy. Fix her, wench!"

"Nothing to fix," soothed Mrs. Davey. "She's just overwhelmed. Which is to be expected after everything that's happened."

"Who can I kill to fix this?" Expression full of thunderclouds, Theodore squinted at the passengers, who chose that moment to leave. Quickly. Some at a run.

"There's no one to kill. Jane just needs a bit of peace and quiet. We should get going. Leave Jane alone with her suitor."

"Just because he's got the locket doesn't give him any rights. They're not married yet." The squint turned in my direction.

"Ozmodeus isn't going to do anything that Jane doesn't want."

"Not reassuring, wench." Whistled through a tight jaw.

Meanwhile, I was fascinated. My father had died at a young age. I'd never gotten to see this kind of repartee between married couples. "I can assure you, sir, that I have nothing but the utmost respect and admiration for Jane."

Davey turned to his wife and, in a loud whisper said, "He called me *sir* again. I think I like it." Formidable beetled brows turned in my direction. "No fornication until marriage."

Yeah, that wasn't happening. A nugget I kept to myself since my future father-in-law still held his sword.

"I'll take good care of Jane." With a nod at them, and a smile at the wink Mrs. Davey tossed at me, I left with Jane, only to find myself mobbed once I got inside the ship. Everyone had something to say.

"Holy shit, we're going to have a pirate in the family!" Jinjur clapped her hands and bounced.

"I could have married a buccaneer," my mother sniffed.

Whereas Jellia arched a brow. "Should I say congratulations?"

"Do you want me to die?" I might plan on mating Jane tonight, but being a man who wanted to keep his head, I'd keep it on the down low until we could do a proper ceremony for her father. He seemed like the type who'd want to walk his daughter down the aisle.

Which meant another wedding cruise. The very idea made me want to groan. Until I looked down at the bundle in my arms.

Worth it.

Given my well-meaning family wouldn't shut up, I finally had to roar at them and stalk through the hush that followed.

"Just like his father," whispered someone.

"A great king," sighed another.

"Until the safari."

My dad had seen a giant bird and went to play with it. Drunk. The ostrich won.

Escaping them all, I noticed that the ship had started moving again, sailing us out of the pirate's reach even as I carried Jane to my bed. I placed her upon the tightly made sheets and then stared at her.

Kept staring.

It didn't take long before she whispered, "Are they all gone?"

"Yes."

"Thank God." She groaned and rolled over, burying her face in a pillow. "I'm sorry. That was such a mess."

"It's actually not that bad. You forget who you're

talking to. In a lion household, drama is a daily thing."

"I grew up with drama. It's exhausting. I miss my parents, but I have to say it's nice to not come home to Dad bellowing that the postman was staring at Mom. Or wondering if he was going to chase off the boy I was tutoring." Even as Jane made these intimate admissions, she wouldn't look at me.

"My mother used to sic my sisters onto my girlfriends."

"Scary."

"No kidding. Although, you don't seem the type to be easily intimidated. And I'll be by your side, helping to handle the drama thrown at us by our families." Reaching, I turned her over. Her bright eyes showed uncertainty.

"What's wrong?" I rubbed her lower lip with my thumb.

"You're a king."

"Yup."

"I'm not even close to being royalty."

"I wouldn't say that. Your father is some kind of big shot at sea." I smiled at her, and yet she still appeared troubled.

She reached out to touch the locket on my chest. "I can't believe you went after it."

"Only way to make sure I stopped the competition. I love you, Jane."

For some reason, that only seemed to make her sadder.

"This is where you say, 'I love you too, Oz, you big, wonderful lion.'"

"I do."

"I hear a *but*…"

"We come from different worlds."

"Which is what makes you perfect." Before she could argue some more, I reminded her how things could be between us by kissing her.

She melted for only a moment before pushing at me. "This isn't what you really want."

"I beg to differ." I moved atop her, letting her feel the evidence of my desire.

"Oh, Oz." The way she sighed my name had me kissing her again. And this time, I didn't give a damn how hard the boat rocked, I wasn't stopping until I'd made Jane mine.

I wasted no time removing the maddening outfit she wore, the long skirt stripped to reveal her legs and the frothy lace panties underneath. The blouse went next, and I made a sound as I saw that she wore nothing over her breasts.

They peeked at me, brazen and tempting. I had no willpower or resistance. I pounced.

The swirl of my tongue across her nipple drew forth a cry from her. A sound that brought a rumble from me.

I scraped the flat edge of my teeth across the tip and then gave it a little bite.

That got my hair tugged. And then almost yanked when I sucked her breasts into my mouth, one by one, pulling and sucking on her flesh. I could gauge her enjoyment by the dig of her nails on my scalp.

The tiny bit of pain only aroused me more. She loved my touch, and I loved the taste of her, so I kept teasing her nipples, switching back and forth between them as she moaned.

The scent of her arousal surrounded me. Sweet honey waiting for a lick. I blazed a trail with my lips and tongue down her body to the pucker of her navel. My bristled jaw stroked against her skin, and a shiver went through her.

She'd be doing more than that before I was done.

My lips kept stroking, a feather-light touch that brought me to a thigh in need of a nibble.

She gasped and giggled.

Unexpectedly ticklish. For some reason, that elated me. I rubbed my unshaven jaw against her next and nipped at her some more, but things turned serious when I chose to stare at her sex. The pink flesh beckoned, her honey making it glisten.

"Pull up your legs," I whispered, blowing the words onto her mound.

Her legs were already spread, but she pulled them up, bending her knees, exposing herself to me.

For me.

I leaned forward and just breathed, the hot air causing her to shiver. The enticing scent of her arousal surrounded me. I needed a taste. I licked her, the decadence of it making me rumble with enjoyment, pleasure she shared.

She sighed my name again. "Oz."

Parting her petals, I lapped and stabbed my tongue into her heat. I could feel her getting close to climax, and I wanted to experience it.

My fingers took the place of my tongue, a pair to stretch her. Hot. Tight. I kept lapping at her sensitive button, teasing it well enough that she gasped and squeezed the thrusting fingers.

When I grabbed her clit with my lips and tugged, her whole body arched off the bed. Her orgasm hit with a hard clamp on my fingers, and I exulted in the waves that pulsed through her body.

But we weren't done yet. I kept thrusting my fingers in, stroking her, making sure to draw out her orgasm, building her to the point where she was panting my name again.

I positioned myself between her legs, the tip of my throbbing cock pressing against her, feeling the heat. I held myself there and whispered, "Jane. Look at me."

Her eyes opened, and she looked upon me, her expression soft, her lips parted.

With our gazes locked, I thrust into her, into that decadent heat. Felt myself fisted by her tight channel.

"I want to stay like this forever," I groaned, holding myself still inside of her, my love for this woman consuming me.

"Forever would be perfect," was her sighed reply.

"Are you sure?" I insisted, nudging just a little with my hips. "We lions tend to mate for life."

"Yes. Yes."

Which was the reply I'd been waiting for.

Even though she gasped and dug her heels into my back, she held my stare, kept it as I began to move inside her. I slammed myself deep—so deep—and ground myself into her, teasing that spot within, the one that triggered her second orgasm.

"Oz." She let go and climaxed, whereas I held on just a bit longer, thrusting in and out, drawing out her pleasure before diving in for a kiss and one last deep stroke.

I came, and as I did, I nipped at her lip. Just a tiny bite. That's all that was needed in that moment. All I needed to make her mine.

We made love a lot over the next few days. Ordering in room service. Ignoring the stop we made at Atlantis to instead cuddle.

I believed that everything was perfect. It never even occurred to me to speak of the future. There would be time enough when we reached land. Except I found myself stunned when I woke to find the ship already docked at our final port, the bed beside me empty, the note she left me maddening.

Thanks for all your help. You really are amazing, but you deserve better than being forced to love a witch because of a spell. I took the locket. You're free.

~Jane Davey

No. No. Oh hell fucking no. She didn't.

I jumped from the bed and took time to only throw on some pants, but by the time I made it to the topmost deck, Jane was already gone.

And my very loud roar made the morning news.

18

JANE: LOVE SPELLS SUCK.

I LEFT. I had to. Despite all the pretty words and epic sex, I knew deep down that Oz didn't really want me. It was the spell in the locket making him do it. Ignoring the fact that magic didn't work on shifters; apparently, the love kind did. Had to be. No way could a guy like Oz love me.

It made me ridiculously sad. Especially since I'd gotten a taste of what love could be. I missed him the moment I left.

I cried as I took the locket I'd brought home with me and soaked it in a brine of vinegar and holy water. It would dissolve any lingering infatuation on his part. Pity, it couldn't do anything about my heart.

It still wanted Oz. Wanted to hear his laughter as he played a naughty prank on his sister. Then his chuckle as he played with my body.

I missed the way he sprawled across the bed and forced me to snuggle him. Such a chore. Despite his devil-may-care attitude, he was actually an intelligent man who'd taken his family's fortune from the brink of middle class and turned it into an empire for…hair products. Mousse. Shampoo. Hairdryers. Once I got over laughing, we actually spent some time discussing ingredients. It seemed that witches did have something to offer a shapeshifter, an intimate knowledge of herbs. Especially a combination I knew that could help reverse balding.

But we'd never collaborate on the revolutionary Janey Tonic. Because I'd left.

Not because I didn't love him. I did with more heart than I thought I had. But that same love wouldn't let me hold on to him because of a spell.

I did the right thing. Which got me a nasty-gram from Lucifer in Hell.

You've just been demoted from the third circle to the fifth. Grow a pair.

~Your Dark Overlord.

PS. Do you have a spell that makes a baby sleep long enough that I can diddle my wife?

I moped.

Alone, I might add. Grandma had apparently rekindled things with Shax. So she was off making my mom a baby sister and me a new aunt. I was sure my therapist could help me bleach that concept from my mind. Eventually.

Since sitting around the house sucked, and I needed a job, I was working on a spell to re-write my ex-boss's memories so I could at least get a decent reference. I neglected my garden due to the downpours. It hadn't stopped raining in Seattle since my return, and probably wouldn't for years to come considering my heavy heart.

A knock on the door had me frowning, especially since I felt that strange quickening of my pulse. Impossible. The spell on the amulet was dead. I glanced over at the bucket just in case.

Nothing from it, and yet I was being tugged in the direction of the door. I approached it, and my palms hovered over the thick wood.

"Who is it?"

"Your mate."

The deep timbre of Oz's voice had me blinking. "How did you find me?"

"I followed my nose."

Flinging open the door, I confronted him. "No way you followed it to me here."

"It helps that I have connections. Although, it wasn't easy. You're unlisted." He loomed in the doorway.

I couldn't help but step back, overwhelmed by

the sight and scent of him. Pure perfection. Longing rose in me, and a faint euphoria that he'd come. Then reality settled in. Remnants of the spell obviously still drove him.

"You shouldn't be here."

"Funny, because I was going to say the same to you."

He stalked into my home, and it filled with his presence.

"Whatever you think you're feeling, it will fade. Soon I would guess since I've dismantled the spell."

"Good. We don't want any misunderstandings. Mundane authorities don't like it when they find their population mauled to death."

"Er. What?" Had he come here to kill me?

"Meaning if that locket ends up in the hands of another, I will get it back. Again and again, until you accept the truth."

"What truth?"

He sighed. "Are you really going to make me spell it out? I love you, Jane Davey."

"You only think you do because of the locket."

"I didn't have the locket when we met. Or the first time we kissed."

"Which is why it was easy for the locket to ultimately twist your emotions," I admitted, not without sadness. "You'll get over it."

"I will not get over it. You are everything I've ever wanted in a woman."

"I'm bitchy."

"Assertive. I happen to like a strong-minded woman."

My heart had started beating again, a flutter of hope inside. But I just had to be me and argue. "I make it rain when I'm sad."

"Then I'll have to make sure you're deliriously happy."

I blinked at him, and it poured outside as tears trembled in my eyes. "Please stop making this harder than it has to be. You don't really love me."

"You are being deliberately dense." He lifted me, hands gripping my forearms and raising me until we were at eye level. "I love you and not because of any damned spell. Or have you forgotten what I am? I'm a lion shifter. I was never charmed into anything."

I pointed out the fallacy with facts. "You said you loved me after you got the locket from the sharks."

"Only because I never had a chance to before. Or have you forgotten our short courtship?"

It was starting to sink in that he wasn't here because of magic. A tremulous smile managed to tug my lips. "I don't know if I'd call that courting."

"Then, perhaps we need to start over. Jane Davey, would you do me the honor of joining me for dinner?"

He still held me, his strength not just in his hands but also in his personality, his character. I stared into his eyes. His beautiful orbs. I looked at his mouth. His decadent lips. "You want us to go out in public?"

"Yes."

I shook my head. "Can't."

He frowned. "Why ever not?"

My lips curved into a smile. "Because the cops in this city give tickets out for acts of indecent exposure."

"Are we going to get indecent?" There was such a hopeful lilt to the query.

"You have no idea." I kissed him. The poor wall in the front hall would never be the same.

Since we had to make up time, we ordered in for the next three days, and it was only as I left him in the shower so one of us could remain clean that I bumped into my grandma walking in through the front door, bright sunlight chasing her.

"Where have you been?" I exclaimed, tucking my towel tighter. "I barely saw you on the ship, and then when the cruise was done, you just left me a note saying you were off on a mission with Shax. What kind of mission?"

Grandma waved a hand. "Not important. I'm guessing by the fact you're not alone that my love spell worked."

I snorted. "Not exactly as you planned. The

locket had nothing to do with it. I ended up with Oz, the lion shifter."

"I thought you might."

I blinked. "Excuse me?"

Grandma tittered. "Oh, please. It was obvious from the moment you met that you were going to end up together."

"Then why didn't he have the locket from the beginning?"

"Because he's a shifter, Jane. Really, use your head. The spell wasn't able to work directly on him, so it created situations to bring you together."

"You mean all those incidents…"

"Brought to you by the wonderful magic of yours truly." Grandma preened. "You're welcome."

But, more importantly, it dispelled any lingering doubt that Oz truly did love me. I really was his mate. I flung my arms around Grandma's neck and hugged her tightly. "Thank you."

The next time I hugged her was at my own wedding, on the same ship where I'd met Oz while anchored over DJ's Locker. My dad walked me down the aisle, scowling every inch of the way. My mother spent the ceremony sobbing from the massive clam shell brought on board specially to keep her moist.

Grandma danced the night away with her demi-demon beau and caught the bouquet.

As for me... I twirled in the arms of my husband —and mate—wearing a brand-new blue dress, borrowed pearl earrings, and an old locket with a picture of Oz and me inside.

Who needed magic when we'd found love?

EPILOGUE

A HONEYMOON on a tropical beach with golden sand.

I snuggled my lover, happy as could be, moonlight bathing my backside. My naked backside.

Finally, I understood why sex in the open could be fun. There was something naughty about it, the wicked exhilaration of possibly getting caught. It reminded me of the hedonistic pleasure I got dancing nude around a fire.

Even better, apparently, my dad now grasped why I'd disliked him and Mom going at it everywhere.

A wave washed over us, gurgling, *"Get a room."*

Maybe later. First, I had to make sure the night we conceived our child under a full moon with both Oz's goddess and my dark lord's blessing was some-

JANE DAVEY'S LOCKET

thing to remember. And how did I know it would happen tonight? Grandma had given me a charm, and I knew better than to doubt her magic.

But I could have killed her when we later found out that it was twins.

This is the end of Jane's story but keep reading for a sneak peek at the next Hell Cruise story.

During the maiden voyage of the Sushi Lover... right about the time Jane was getting ready for that first breakfast.

Sasha, a passenger on a cruise, woke up in her room aboard the ship. Hungover.

Still fully dressed atop the comforter but wearing something new.

A ring.

On her left hand. The stone set within the white metal was huge!

It was then that she had a brief recollection of saying "I do" in that all-night chapel beside the casino and kissing a dude that had her hyperventilating.

"Oh, dear God. I think I got married."

What Sasha doesn't know, but is about to find out, is that during that drunken wedding,

SHE BECAME *THE BRIDE OF THE SEA MONSTER*...AND IT WILL TAKE A WHOLE LOT OF CONVINCING BEFORE SHE'LL ACCEPT HIS LOVE.

For more fun in the Welcome to Hell world see EveLanglais.com

www.ingramcontent.com/pod-product-compliance
Ingram Content Group UK Ltd.
Pitfield, Milton Keynes, MK11 3LW, UK
UKHW042001230426
12048UKWH00009B/480